Beneath the Urban Stars

Beatrice Lebrun

BENEATH THE URBAN STARS

© 2026 Beatrice Lebrun

All rights reserved.

No part of this book may be reproduced or transmitted in any form or by any means, electronic or mechanical, including photocopying, recording, or by an information storage and retrieval system - except by a reviewer who may quote brief passages in a review to be printed in a magazine or newspaper - without permission in writing from the publisher.

This is a work of fiction. Names, characters, places, and incidents are either the product of the author's imagination or used fictitiously. Any resemblance to actual persons, living or dead, events, or locales is entirely coincidental.

ISBN 979-8-9991162-3-9 (ebook) - ISBN 979-8-9991162-4-6 (paperback) - ISBN 979-8-9991162-5-3 (hardcover)

Cover design, illustrations, formatting, and layout by Beatrice Lebrun.

Edited by Midnight Markups LLC

First edition, 2026

Beneath the Urban Stars

Beatrice Lebrun

CONTENT WARNINGS

This story contains themes that may be distressing to some readers, including:

Obsessive limerence

Allusions to past suicide attempts (not specified)

Sleep paralysis

Romanticization of dangerous behavior

Hallucinations

Derealization

Non-specific mental illness

HPD

BDP

Depression

Suicidal ideation

Please read with care. Your safety comes first.

If you ever need to step away, that's okay.

This story unfolds like a dream, it can wait until you're ready.

This book is for you.
You, who learned to doubt if love would ever find you.
You, who thought you had to hide yourself to deserve it.
You, who found it easier to live in dreams, because reality was too much.
I wrote this thinking of you.

I'm glad you're here.

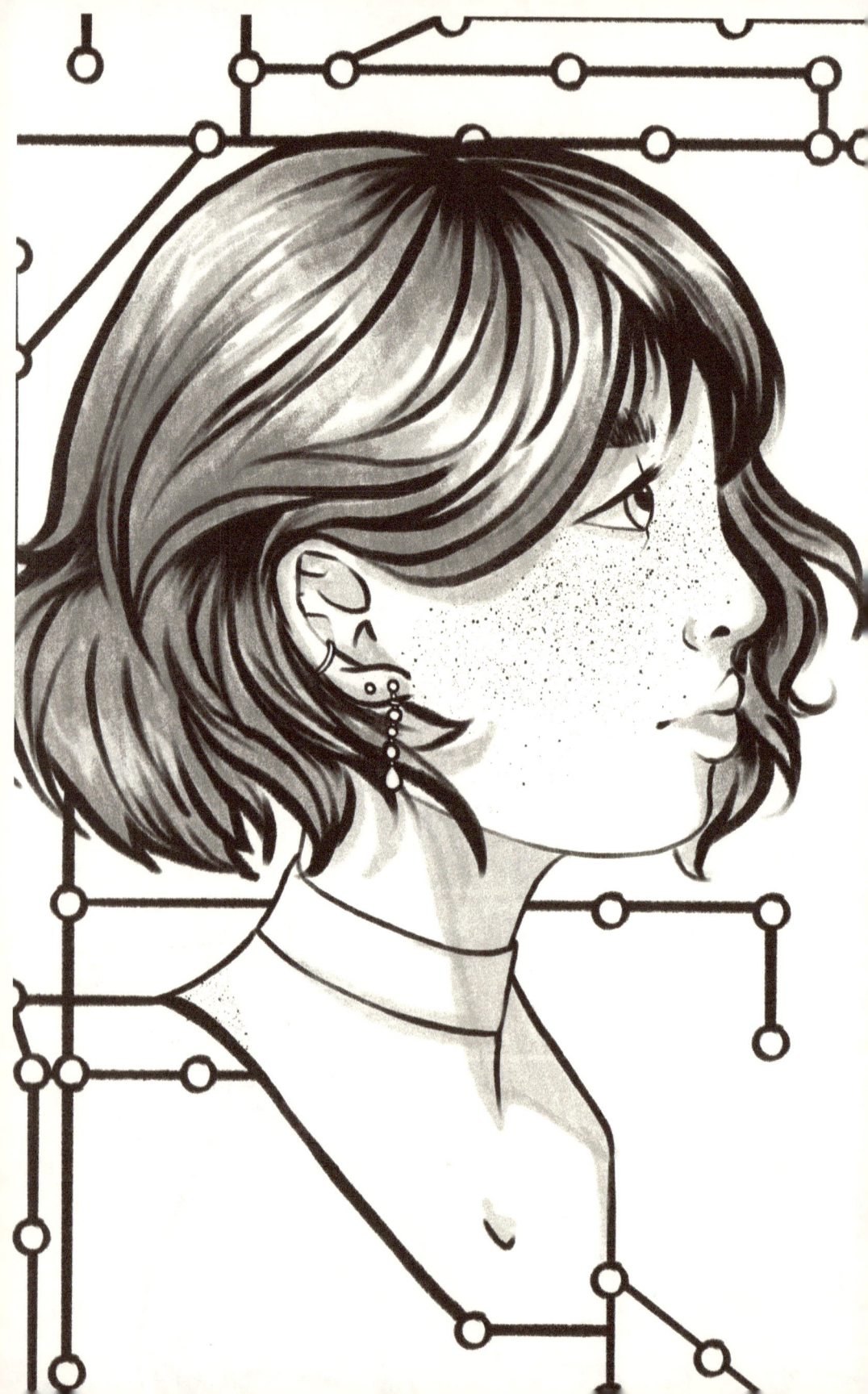

1
Craving Connection

When I was little, I dreamed about growing up. I imagined myself being a *successful adult* as soon as I turned 21; I truly believed I would have my life all figured out by then.

I wish I could go back.

It's funny how there's this expectation of having your life completely solved by the flip of a switch, just by a date in the calendar changing.

How ironic.

Adult life hit me like a moving train, work consumed my entire existence, and socializing started seeming more and more like one of those unattainable goals you set for yourself when the clock strikes midnight on New Year's.

The **bus** became my home, my life. I never learned how to drive, and living and working on opposite sides of the city would do that to you. It was always filled with anonymous strangers, coming and going, with tired and miserable expressions.

Like me.

I tried my best for a while, and I've always been kind of desperate to be noticed. To be adored. To be *special.*

So I made a conscious effort to wake up earlier than usual, do my hair and makeup, fix my clothing. Be who I had always aspired to be, someone who would turn heads by just passing by.

Fake it 'till you make it, I guess.

I lived that lie for as much as my brain managed to keep it going. Pretending to be confident turned into almost a second skin, dry and patchy. Peeling.

Every single day for as long as I could. Wake up. Get ready. Smile. Try to make my eyes sparkle. Swivel my hips a little more. Flip my hair the right amount of times. Laugh just a tad louder than I should. Anything. Everything.

It gets old.

It destroys your brain.

Eventually, I stopped trying. Why would I keep it going when it was such a lost cause?

Only one thing stayed consistent. I kept existing on the **bus** more than at my regular home, this time with eye bags and whatever concealer I could put on in 5 minutes to try to keep my freckles in check. I was still looking for something, I won't lie. But it seemed worthless.

Looking for adventure, for trouble maybe, or love, or whatever plot in whatever movie was streaming at the moment.

Something.

Anything at all.

The days all seemed to *blendtogether*, one indistinguishable *fromthe* next. It was like my life had become a never-ending bus ride, with each day passing by in a blur, leaving me feeling like I was just going through the motions of barely existing.

The same thing over and over. Every *wordstuck toeachother* in my brain. I became used to losing track of time, of sense, of reality. It was like my life had become a never-ending bus ride, with each day *passingby inablur* and leaving me feeling like I *wasjust goingthroughthe* motions.

The same thing over and over.

Every *wordstuck toeachother* in my brain.

I became used to losing track of time.

Of sense.

Of reality.

Deja vú.

But then.

One day.

A sliver of hope with black hair adorned by silver strands.

Him.

He appeared out of nowhere. At first, I barely noticed his existence. Somehow, he seemed to always be there, in every single **bus** ride. Sitting in the exact same seat, next to the exact same window. There was something different about him, like he was supposed to be the main character, and we were all part of the background.

He felt so out of place, like reality almost bent for him to walk through it. Something, that something about him drew me like a magnet in ways words can't describe. His eyes always immersed in that notebook he seemed to be attached to almost by his own skin. Scribbling, drawing, writing, I had no clue.

Every time I tried to move closer I would freeze, like this supernatural force would wash over me and make me forget how to even breathe.

He terrified me for reasons that I couldn't explain.

So out of place in the most perfect way, every time I looked in his direction, my heart would stop for a second, and my entire body would start to tremble. So many times I tried to lock eyes with him, but he was content to exist in his own bubble, where only he and his notebook existed. But I kept trying.

And trying.

And trying.

I knew that if he saw me, even for a split second, he would understand. He would feel what I felt. It was almost supernatural, and I had no proof, but without even hearing his voice, I knew we were connected.

Tied by an invisible string.

His presence was comforting, more than just the mere idea of breaking the stickiness of the boredom that everyone else carried with themselves. My mouth would start to dry out, or salivate, or both. My skin would flutter. I would lose balance and all sense of reason.

I forgot how to breathe a couple of times.

And then he would leave, and my entire world would crumble once again.

I cried more than once, wanting to throw myself out of the window to follow him. Scream a name I didn't even know. Every time he went down those steps and exited through those doors, he would take a part of me with him.

What was it about him that had the power to shatter my entire reality just by breathing the same air as me?

I would fantasize about the sound of his voice and the things he would like to eat, about what kept him awake at night. Wonder if he even liked girls. If he even liked girls like me.

He had to, because we were connected.

Right?

It was insanity, I knew it. Probably anyone who looked at my face for longer than two seconds would have known it too. But I didn't care. I had already given up on being attractive for anyone else but him.

Him.

I needed to do something about him.

It was almost like my life depended on it.

2
Cringe-Worthy Encounter

There he was, with his eyes almost piercing those pages that seemed to absorb him so much.

Even from a distance, I could almost smell the graphite of his mechanical pencil with every stroke. I had never wanted so badly to be a piece of paper as I did at that instant.

The **bus** was jam-packed, and the world seemed to be shrouded in an imperceptible veil, like it usually happened whenever I noticed his presence. The streetlights flickered outside, and buildings loomed like shadowy giants, almost shivering in anticipation.

Like me.

I think I wouldn't have been able to stand up if I wasn't already doing so, and trapped in between the scramble of people trying to fit into the small **bus** hallway like sardines. Because that day, for the first time since he had come into my life, I was closer than ever.

My body knew it; the giant freezing sweat drops falling from my forehead were a clear indication . A wave of nausea came and went every time I looked directly at him. And he wouldn't look at me. Because he was too entranced with that notebook.

What was in it?

I fought my brain and reflexes and tried to extend my neck as much as I could, to catch a glimpse of the thing that had him so mystified. But the **bus** jumped, turned, shook. The words were blurry and the drawings confusing. Yet, I was so close I could smell his hair.

Bitter. Slightly bitter.

I felt it in my mouth.

Like unsweetened tea.

Electricity ran down my spine and the underside of my nails started itching. If only I could extend my arms just a bit, I would be able to touch him, to feel the softness of those black and silver strands that had been driving me crazy for days.

Weeks.

Months.

Something in my gut told me he was trouble, maybe that's the reason I liked him so much. The more my instincts were trying to convince me to forget about him, the more I felt drawn to him. A sensation I had felt many times before, especially when I was a child and I was doing something I wasn't supposed to.

It's funny how those feelings seem to disappear as you grow up.

Until they come back twice as strong one day.

I couldn't move my arm; once again, that indescribable force of the universe trying to keep us apart. But I leaned a tiny bit, and a little bit more after that. My vision became blurry, I still couldn't understand any of the words. The bus kept shaking and turning and jumping.

I rubbed my eyes and tried again. I was close enough, nothing made sense. Everything else around me was fine; I could see it in perfect detail.

But that notebook, those scribbles on it.

Wavering.

Like an illusion.

The bus kept shaking and turning and jumping.

Until it suddenly stopped.

Abruptly.

So abruptly, it propelled me to the front, and my chest clashed against the metal bar.

Gasping for air, I looked around, but everyone else seemed unfazed. Nondescript faces with their stares lost in the distance, ignoring everything that was going next to them. Some weren't even holding the rails, they just stood there with vacant eyes. Like zombies.

A groan next to me brought my attention back. The guy I had been admiring from afar, right next to me.

Him.

He was leaning forward, so I could only see the top of his head. The temptation to touch him took hold of me. How would the texture of his jacket feel? The skin on his neck?

Until I felt a tug under my foot that made me realize why he was leaning like that in the first place.

I moved to the side, still completely stunned, and he just took his notebook and began to check it, probably to see if it was dirty or something.

'Look up,' I thought while almost stabbing the nape of his neck with my stare. 'Just look at me!'

He muttered something under his breath, too low for me to make out what it was, and then stretched his neck while rubbing it.

So close.

'Just turn a bit more.'

My mouth was dry, and I had to grab the seats on both sides to prevent myself from completely collapsing. I opened my lips, and no sound came out of them. Clearing my throat, I tried again.

And again.

And again.

Until finally:

"Hey! Are you— are you okay?!" My voice came out three pitches higher than it normally was, and I choked right in the middle of it, but at least it was *something*.

The windows in the room started to fog up, and I got a chill down my spine. The pressure on my chest became stronger with every breath. Unease, that thing in my gut trying to scream as loud as it could. It was like time had stopped, and I was just there, holding my breath, waiting for something to happen. I was positive I would faint any second then.

But I needed to hold it, at least for a minute longer.

I *needed* to at least hear his voice.

Maybe he hadn't heard me in the first place?

Then, he choked.

The beautiful boy finally cast his gaze upon me, his piercing grey eyes demolishing me entirely. And then choked and gasped for air and started almost coughing his lungs out. His face distorted between confusion and fear, and I literally just wanted to die. To jump from the bus window and hopefully be run over by a car.

"What's wrong?" I hear myself saying, way too quiet and meek to sound like my real voice, like a desperate cry.

His lips trembled, and I couldn't help but extend one of my hands towards him. Maybe he needed help.

I just needed to know what his skin felt like.

"WHAT THE ACTUAL FUCK?!" His voice was loud and probably as broken as mine had sounded a second ago.

He leaned back so abruptly that I thought he was going to smash his head against the window. His eyes fluttered around us, and his breath started becoming faster and faster.

I couldn't move; the sensation on my chest was taking over the rest of my body. What was there in his eyes?

Disgust?

Anger?

Horror?

The words again couldn't leave my lips, but I was able to mouth them. He stared at them for a second, it made my body shiver. His beautiful grey eyes, finally paying some attention to me.

But at what cost?

"What's wrong?" I finally said, my voice barely above a whisper. My response sounded far away from wherever I was, like a mirage.

"Can you... see me?" He spoke hesitantly. It seemed like he had chosen his words carefully, intentionally.

His eyes started darting around us again, almost like he was trying to find something only he could see. His voice was melodic and raspy and so beautiful. His face so delicate and angular. His eyelashes so long.

His... words were so weird.

'What did he say?'

"Are you... Did you hear me? *Can* you hear me? Can you *see* me?" He sounded cautious, scared, like he had broken an unspoken rule by even acknowledging me.

"What's happening? Did you hit your head?" My voice trembled. I could see the color drain from his face as my words reached him.

I tried to move forward and put my hands on his shoulders, but he seemed to try to melt through the wall behind him.

The bus shook and turned and almost forced me out of the row of seats we were sharing, but I held on for dear life because I wasn't about to lose my only chance of trying to have at least a normal conversation with the one person that has been running around my brain for hell knew how long already.

"Am I in early this time?" he muttered to himself, still looking straight into my eyes. "Is *this* supposed to mean something?"

I was too stunned to speak, too confused to move.

My mind racing with questions.

His hand approached the end of my hair, and my entire world collapsed in an instant. His fingers were so close to my lower jaw that I could feel the tiny hairs on my skin almost grazing them. I tried to muster up the courage to speak, but my throat felt dry and constricted.

It was like all the words I had ever known suddenly disappeared from my mind once more.

He was so close.

So close.

I tried to flutter my eyelashes and smile, but my face contorted in ways I couldn't distinguish. If only I could move just a tiny bit forward, we would be even closer. And closer. And closer.

His breath smelled like a new book right after picking it up for the first time. I needed to read him, to lose myself in him. Maybe he was feeling it too, maybe that's why he was acting so strange.

Maybe he felt that same constriction in his chest.

Maybe he was trying to fight a world that was trying to pull us apart before we had even met.

Maybe.

Maybe.

Maybe.

"Redhead, huh? Weird."

'Again. What did he just say?'

"Weird? What do you mean weird?" I jolted back and suddenly all the energy I didn't have came back to me. He withdrew his hand like I had shocked him, or burned it, or both. "What's wrong with you?!"

The bus stopped.

It didn't slow down, didn't turn, give any sign. Just stopped.

I almost fell again, he held on to one of the seats and then stood up, didn't even bother to respond. He passed by me without even asking me to move, almost like he assumed he would go right through me.

Was he smiling?

When I realized he was trying to get down, I tried to follow him, but the flurry of people that had been almost completely immobile during our whole exchange started trying to push and pull and get down again. He couldn't leave, not like this. I felt like throwing up again.

"Hey!" I raised my voice, hopefully loud enough for him to hear me, barely able to breathe.

"Hey!" He responded when he reached the front door and looked back with a smile. I was still trapped in the crowd. "Nice meeting you, *redhead!*" And stepped out of the bus with a chuckle.

I fell on the seat next to me.

♥ 15 ♥

He smiled at me.

He smiled at me!

The world slowed down, and the only thing that mattered was the lingering sound of his voice. His smile. His eyes finally noticing me.

Me, a complete stranger.

One more in the pile of bodies in their commute, barely existing.

He *knew* I was special.

I leaned back and gazed through the window, trying to find him, but the fog covered everything and I could barely see the streetlights, twinkling like fireflies in a cloud of mist.

Beautiful fireflies, dancing, waiting.

There was something else.

Something poking at my butt. The seat? His seat. His notebook? His notebook!

I held it in my hands like the most precious treasure I had ever found. The one thing that kept his gaze from me for so long. Mine.

He had to come back to me, even if it was just to get it back.

Maybe it was the key for my second chance, to get him to like me.

To get him to love me.

So I flipped through the pages and noticed the same scribbles as before, some sketches here and there, some dates even. Not a single word, at least not an intelligible one. It didn't even seem to be in another language. Just pure gibberish. It seemed to mock me.

Was I going insane?

I looked outside one more time, the streetlights gone, the fog consuming everything around. Dark, eerie.

And then I realized.

I had completely forgotten what stop I was supposed to get off.

3
Just Can't Forget

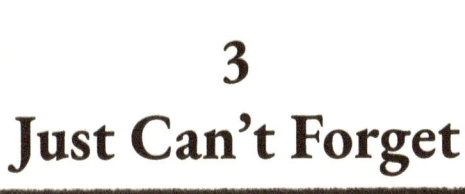

The night before I met her was already really fucking weird.

The air had this thick, uncomfortable texture that stuck to my lungs with every inhale. Something was going on, I could feel it in my bones, pulsating right in the middle of my forehead.

Even before the **bus**, my brain was already starting to untangle on its own, the tiredness of the day forcing the walls down, whether I liked it or not. I had to use the last willpower I had on my way back from work just to not blow my cover. I directed all my energy into pretending I was one of them.

Normal. Accepted.

I had been dealing with it my entire life. The colors, the people, the sounds. All those overwhelming details that I had learned to tolerate would become nightmares. The more tired I was, the less brain energy I had to combat my instinct to run away.

The burden of existence.

That's why I liked the **bus** so much. It was my place to breathe, to relax, to finally be able to think. There, I didn't have to pretend to smile because I knew it was the right moment to do so, or worry about the way everyone around me was perceiving me. I could just disappear into myself, become whoever I wanted to be at that moment.

I could let the mask go and be the messy, weird, anxious, horny, and fucking stressed-out guy I really was on the inside.

There I didn't exist, or maybe where the others who didn't do so?

It was a sacred place at a sacred time, where I could tune out the rest of the world, free from arbitrary norms and idiotic consequences.

So that night came in, like every single other one. And I grabbed my notebook, and my mechanical pencil, and started drawing and writing and...

And then she spoke.

Even afterwards, her voice still felt like an echo bouncing against the walls of my brain. It cracked my thoughts into pieces, screamed at my memories without words.

Over, and over, and over again.

She haunted me even after I had left.

Why?

I didn't even remember what happened next, and yet the memory of her was so vivid it almost burned. The freckles decorating her skin and her pupils so dilated she looked unreal.

Beyond comprehension.

What the fuck was going on?

The rest of the night was awful. I kept waking up in cold sweats without making sense as to why, like my brain had finally decided to empty itself and I hadn't gotten the memo.

Her eyes seemed to pierce through my soul even after hours had passed and she was long gone. A wave of nausea overcame me every time she came to mind.

Why?

My stomach was short-circuiting, my heart was collapsing, my intuition was begging me to stop.

But I couldn't.

I couldn't stop thinking about her.

Even after night turned into day and I had to force myself to be a member of society again, our conversation still replayed in my head against my will. Instead of focusing on work, I kept trying to analyze every word and microexpression I could find in her face.

There was something there, something about her.

"Who's that?" Leo's voice shattered my internal processing.

I looked around, trying to remember where I was and what was going on.

Work. Focus.

I stared at the computer in front of me, the phone that thankfully hadn't been ringing, the piece of recycled paper on the desk. The graphite lines, working together to make the same image that had been plaguing my mind for the entire day.

"Someone I met the other day," I answered, hiding the drawing. And it felt like a lie.

"She's kinda cute," he teased with a smile, before going back to his desk next to mine.

He was as cute as her though, but I would've never admitted that out loud.

'Too unprofessional', my brain whispered at me. So I bit my tongue like every time I had considered for a second on complimenting him, or inviting him out, or letting myself smile way too much around him.

"She is, I guess. But it's whatever, it's not like I'm going to see her again or anything," and that somehow also tasted like a lie.

I tried so hard the rest of the day.

Tried to work, to focus.

She wouldn't leave me alone.

Every time I had a second of free will my thoughts would get tangled in her, I tried to throw away the portrait I had made but couldn't bear to do so. There was something there, something I wasn't seeing.

I needed time to sit down, to breathe, to be by myself and think.

I needed the **bus.**

My heart was racing when it was finally time to leave work, almost with desperation. The little bits of food I ate were threatening to escape almost as quickly as I was running down the stairs.

I stopped myself. And forced my feet to walk at a normal pace.

Because I was normal, and normal people didn't run down the stairs after work like that.

Normal people didn't become obsessed with mirages either, but no one else had to know about it.

It was idiotic! Like a stupid teenager after the first time they realize they like someone, anyone at all.

Was that what I was feeling?

Love?

It didn't really fucking feel like it. It also didn't make any sense at all.

Feelings towards... who?

What?

Redhead. Freckles. Dilated pupils. Smile.

Anxiety seemed to crawl through my body like a swarm of insects, one by one breaking my pores apart. I needed to get out of the way of the people, I was so close to finally having a breather.

Of course I wasn't.

Getting home didn't do shit either.

"You need to stop yourself from going down that rabbit hole, man.

Once you do, you know you'll be gone." Perfect, I had started to talk out loud once again.

I forced myself to close the search page and, almost like it had a mind of its own, my hand decided to take the drawing out of my pocket.

She was smiling, mocking me.

What the fuck did it all mean?

Not even in the quiet of my apartment could I have peace, she kept following me with those eyes. Her voice whispered puzzles I didn't even have the pieces for.

I made dinner, took a shower, screamed at the walls.

Nothing worked to kick her out.

I needed the **bus**.

After what seemed like an eternity, it finally arrived.

The relief that washed over me when I finally found myself surrounded by those seats was overwhelming. I walked to my regular seat and for a second just stayed there, taking in the blurry view of the buildings passing by. The quiet hum of the lights, the anonymity of it all.

Finally able to breathe again, I started the routine I had come up with since I was a teenager. Closed my eyes, tried to go over the entire day in my head, let my brain get back to thinking instead of being in automatic mode.

Her.

I kept seeing her face everywhere.

And something was off.

My hands were... empty?

It always took a while to regain that lucidity, to understand my surroundings. Something, something was missing between my hands. I looked around, at everyone around me, with their vacant stares.

Something.

Something that was mine.

My bag? No

My phone? I never brought it here.

My notebook?

My notebook!

I threw myself to the floor, looking underneath all the seats around me. Checked in between the cushions while my chest was threatening to suffocate me. My notebook. My notebook. How was that possible?

It didn't make any sense.

I always had it, every single time.

How was I supposed to even process my day? My anger? My fears? I needed to draw, to write. It was my sacred process. My sacred routine. My sacred bus ride.

"I'm sorry about yesterday," the voice pierced through my ears. "Are you looking for this? You left it here."

There she was, the face was no longer made of graphite. The eyes were so full of light, reflective even. The mouth twisting into something in between excitement and shame.

So realistic.

How was that possible?

I opened my mouth but couldn't make a sound. My legs began to shake and I sat down before they were able to give out completely. She stood there, breathing heavily, nervous, almost panicking.

The notebook.

My notebook.

I took it from her hands with a gentleness I didn't know I had and the immediate relief made everything feel alright for a moment.

For a moment, my fingers grazed hers. Warm, soft.

Alive.

She looked so real my heart cracked. It felt fucked up, unfair.

What was this twisted game my brain was playing?

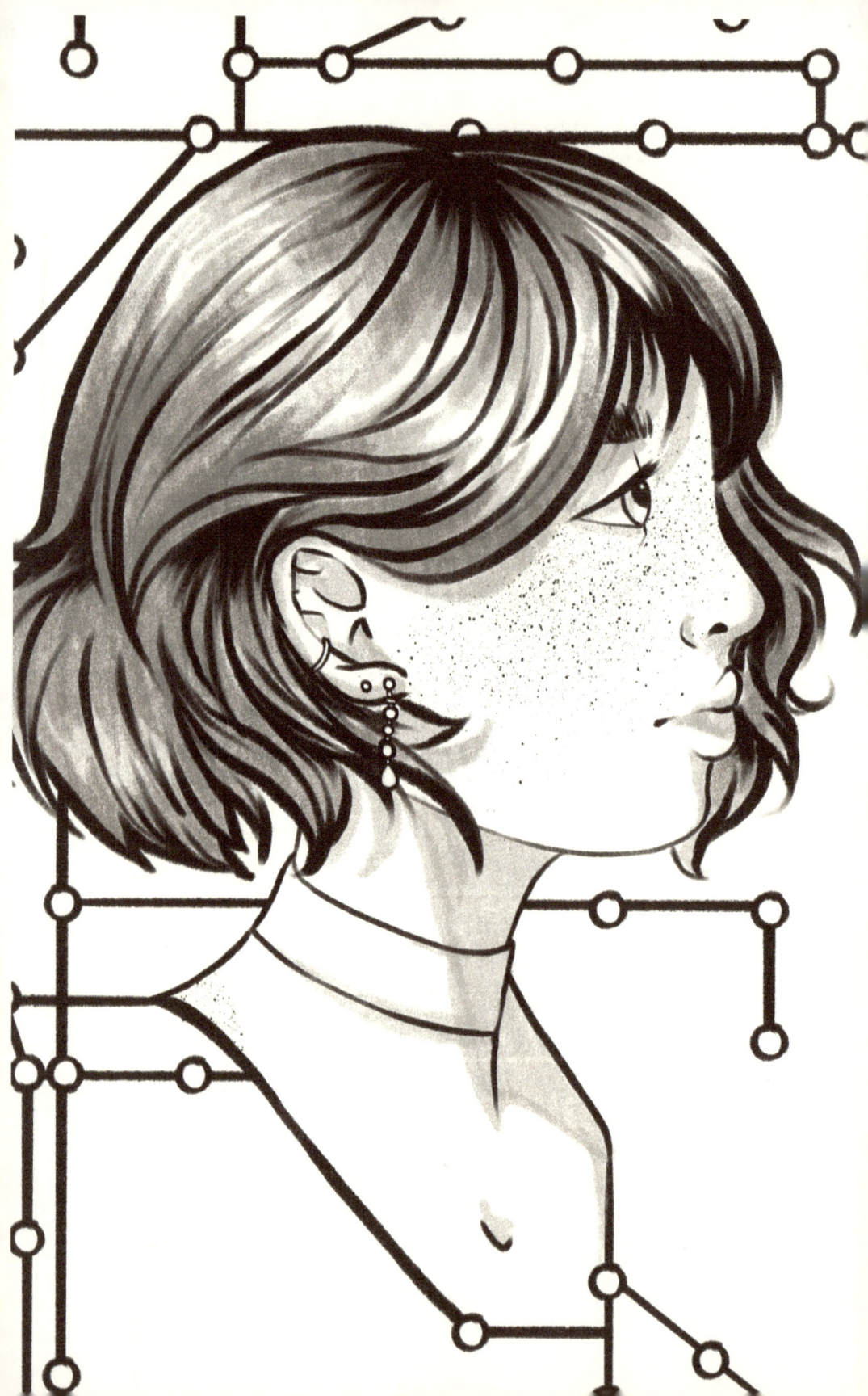

4
Confronting the Impossible

Not even the deep lethargy I felt would have been enough to make me let go of this notebook. I ran my fingertips over the texture of the cover again and again and smiled.

'He'll come back, he has to,' I repeated to myself over and over, in a whisper. 'He's obsessed with this notebook. Even if he didn't need the bus, he has to know he left it here'

Even though *here* was uncertain.

The days had been blurry lately, confusing, boring. Seeing him was my only consolation against the monotony. I couldn't remember the last time I checked the date, or what day of the week it was.

Or what I had for breakfast that morning, or even if it was day or night.

Or when I got off the bus the day before.

Or when I got on that day.

Anyway, monotony.

Nothing else was important other than the notebook after all, my key to him. I tried to find a single word I could understand, but the drawings were the only thing that made sense. Maybe the scribbles were some kind of shorthand, like the things that doctors use and no one else understands.

Would he be a doctor? He didn't look like the type.

But, what did he look like anyway?

Like an artist, a poet of some kind or maybe an actor. He looked like he was beyond a normal job, a normal *anything*. That was one of the things I loved the most about him, everything made him seem so ethereal, so above the conformity of everything I had almost been forced to live through my entire life.

I ran my fingers through the pages, coming back to the one that called to me for reasons I couldn't explain. A big, red STOP sign in a sea of otherwise greys and blacks and blues. It seemed to mock me, to try to communicate with me somehow. It was the only pop of color in the entire notebook and it made my stomach churn, similarly to how I felt every time I locked eyes with him.

Maybe he had done it on purpose, left it for me to find and interpret it somehow. He looked like the type.

The type to speak in riddles and hidden messages.

"Can you... see me?" His voice reverberated inside my skull like a ping pong ball.

It was a secret message, obviously, some sort of code he desperately wanted me to crack. Could've even been related to the STOP sign. But, what did it even mean?

"Are you... Did you hear me? *Can* you hear me? Can you *see* me?"

He could've just hit his head, of course.

But I did hear him, I did see him. I saw him way before he even knew I existed.

That's what that had to mean, he understood I saw him more than anyone else in this **bus**, probably anyone else in his life. He knew I was watching, he felt me as much as I felt him. Because we were connected somehow, and at that moment, he knew too.

That was the only logical explanation.

I looked up, his image was so ingrained in my brain that I could almost see him, standing there, looking around. Sitting down, staring at his hands. Panicking, confused.

It was...

It was him!

I sprinted towards him, clutching the notebook for dear life, not caring that the **bus** was moving and I almost face planted the floor.

"I'm sorry about yesterday," I said, trying my best not to pant. "Are you looking for this? You left it here."

Every single muscle in my face contracted, trying to make me smile. It hurt, almost as much as my chest.

He opened his mouth in shock and I slowly started to relax. Once he grabbed the notebook, he looked at me like I had saved his life. And I suddenly felt more alive than I had for days.

But then his eyes shifted, something else dimmed the sparkle. Sadness, pain.

He sat down and I took my chance to sit next to him. Speaking was still hard in his presence, but I still tried to gather all my energy to do so. He beat me to it.

"I don't get it," he said, looking *past* me. "Did I do something specific to trigger it?"

It could be his thing, speaking only in riddles. The floor below me started shaking slowly and I had to hold on to the seat in front of me for a bit of stability.

"I'm sorry, I'm really trying to understand but I—" I started, but a second afterwards his empty hand was touching my hair and I started to melt. It felt like a feather brushing against my cheek, the warmth radiating from his skin made me dizzy.

He leaned all the way towards me, too close for a stranger to do so, his gaze almost studying me. This was exactly what I wanted and more, and yet I froze and felt like throwing up again. He was too close for breathing, too close for thinking. Too close for comfort.

"You just look so *real*," he whispered as he played with the strands between his fingers. "Even the outfit makes sense. This is nuts."

I could almost see the cogs turning inside his brain. Intrigued. Confused. A bit delusional?

"Are there any pills that you have to take and forgot or something?" The question sounded rougher than what I expected coming from my lips, I cleared my throat, trying to tremble a bit less than before. "I take a few, maybe it's the same ones, I probably have some in my purse."

I sounded like a bitch. He probably thought I was one.

"I mean, sometimes when I forget to take mine I also act weird like this." Every single word that came out of my mouth just kept making everything worse. "Not that you're acting weird. You're not that weird. Well, a little bit but I think that's okay. I'm weird too." I needed to shut up immediately. "So, what do you take?"

My hands automatically went to my side, but couldn't feel my purse. I looked around, trying to have it save me from this absolute embarrassment. My lungs started filling up faster and faster, I know what would happen if I didn't calm down immediately.

'My purse, my purse.'

I couldn't see the seat where I was before, but for sure I had left it there. It was probably gone by then, someone would've probably stolen it. My phone was in my pocket, but my wallet, and my pills, and...

"Pills? Wait, is this what this whole thing is about?" His voice brought me back. "Is this my brain trying to tell me I need to take my medication?!"

He looked disappointed.

I wanted to go get my purse.

"I'm sorry, I have to—" I got up and tried to glance at the other side of the **bus**, his hand wrapped around my wrist and I screamed.

"I'm sorry! I'm not used to this. Don't go, I just need to get used to it." He closed his eyes, he seemed more like thinking out loud than trying to make conversation. "*Ugh...* Redhead? No, that's not right. I should give you a name."

"A name? I *have* a name!" I shook my wrist but he was holding on to it. Hard. "It's Chiara, you could've just asked. You flirt really weird."

Were the windows of the bus always this foggy?
Were they related to the pressure on my chest?
To the pain on my side?

"Why would you already have a name if I made you?" He finally let go, looking at me like I was a ghost.

His eyes widened like he was trying to understand something beyond his comprehension. And my chest kept aching and I knew if it kept going, I would be out of air soon.

"Are you okay? Are you self aware? Is that why?" Every single word he said made everything worse. My muscles stiffened, my skull was threatening to smash my brain like a grapefruit. His hand tried to come closer again but I growled.

"Listen I have no clue how to talk to dream people, okay? Usually they just act like this!" He shouted, also desperate, pointing at everyone around us.

The ones that behaved like zombies.

Devoid of life, of light.

Something pushed me back to the seat, like invisible hands trying to restrain me.

"You're insane," I heard the words come from my lips but didn't register them until seconds after it came through my ears. "What's that supposed to mean?"

I looked around almost against my will. At the foggy windows and the streetlights that looked so similar to yesterday's, and the day before, and the one before that one.

At the seats, at the people.

The air felt charged, dense, unreal.

Maybe everyone had gone crazy.

With more effort than it should've taken, I stood up and started walking through the middle aisle.

"Excuse me" I said to the woman right in front of us. "Excuse me?" I got so close to her face I should've felt her breath. I even nudged her a little.

"Excuse me?!" I repeated to the man next to her.

And the people on the other side.

And the kids right in front of them.

"Chiara?" The guy's voice sounded like it came from a radio in a distant room.

I pushed a girl and she ragdolled to the seat next to her, then came back to the exact position she was before, like a video in reverse. She didn't even bother to turn around and look at me.

"What's happening?" I whispered to nothing and no one. Freezing cold sweat started sliding down my side. "Where is this **bus** going?"

"Chiara?" He sounded closer this time.

I couldn't remember the last time I checked the date, or what day of the week it was.

Or what I had for breakfast that morning, or even if it was day or night.

Or when I got off the bus the day before.

Or when I got on that day.

Every single time my mind tried to wander, it started fading away. I tried to chase memory after memory, but they were too fast for me.

I couldn't remember anything that didn't happen in that **bus.**

I couldn't remember anything that didn't happen in that moment.

I couldn't remember.

I couldn't remember.

I couldn't remember.

I couldn't remember.

I couldn't remember.

I couldn't remember.

I couldn't remember.

I couldn't remember.

I couldn't remember.

I couldn't remember.

I couldn't remember.

I couldn't remember.

I couldn't remember.

I couldn't remember.

I couldn't remember.

"Chiara!" He was next to me now.

I turned around and saw the panic in his eyes, probably a reflection of how I looked. He became blurry and then focused again. I couldn't stop swiveling, he held onto my shoulders to help my balance. My head started twitching. Air. Breathing was hard. So hard. My chest. So much pain. My skull, my head.

My brain.

"I'm sorry. I didn't... You're *real?*" He caught himself. "You're real! My name is Jasper, ok? And I need you to calm down right now."

He looked around, scared, pleading.

I didn't care about what he needed.

I *needed* to get out.

I ran to the front.

The stupid part of me really thought it was true, that I wouldn't find a driver in their seat. Ridiculous. Insane. I just needed to get down and would finish walking. It had been a mistake, that was exactly what I deserved for being this obsessed with a stranger that apparently had turned out to be a madman.

"Hi, sorry," my voice cracked, the driver turned to look at me for way longer than she should have. "When's the next stop?"

Her head slowly went back to the position it was before.

Like a video in reverse.

No answer.

I tapped on the thick layer of translucent plastic that separated us. One, two times. She turned to me again.

"Excuse me!" I repeated, a little louder this time. "Can you tell me what the next stop is?"

Sweat poured down my face, drenching my forehead and cheeks with sticky droplets. My tears started mixing with them, forming salty rivulets that streamed down my face. It couldn't be. Maybe I was the one who had missed her pills. Maybe it was me who was insane.

Maybe it was all a nightmare.

The driver's head went back a second time, like it was made of rubber.

I screamed.

I did so until my legs gave in and dropped to the floor.

I did so until my throat hurt so much I felt like it would bleed.

I did so all the way down the steps to the door.

I did so while banging at it, trying to open it.

I did so until I felt his arms wrapping around me.

"Chiara," this time his voice sounded gentle, soothing. "We're dreaming. We're the only real things in this place."

5
Jumping Into the Unknown

Fuck.

Fuck. Shit. Fuck. Shit. Shit. Fucking shit. What the fuck!?

I just... It never...

I needed to breathe.

It wasn't real. It wasn't real. Why did it feel so real when it wasn't?

She was warm to the touch and could hold up entire conversations, and looked so scared and confused, and I just didn't get it.

I sprinted towards her and wrapped her in my arms. I needed silence to focus. I needed to think for more than a second. She froze, but at least didn't try to get out of the embrace.

She was still warm to the touch.

Could she really be... real?

I bit my tongue and tried to control my breathing. Nothing happened; at least she wasn't screaming anymore.

"Chiara," I whispered, afraid that entertaining the idea of her being an actual, real-life person would send me down the deep end. "We're dreaming. We're the only real things in this place."

She nodded, sobbing, defeated.

I bit my tongue again, trying to will her to do anything crazy, out of character. Jump on one foot, sing happy birthday, change the color of her eyes.

Still nodding.

Still sobbing.

Still defeated.

The taste of something that vaguely resembled blood filled my mouth.

Still nodding.

Still sobbing.

Still defeated.

Fuck.

This was really happening.

I wiped my mouth with my sleeve, but nothing stained it, of course, because none of this was fucking real.

Except for her.

I half-dragged her, half-carried her to one of the front seats. She couldn't stop shaking. My head was killing me as it still tried to piece together this mess. Never in all the years I had been researching lucid dreaming and astral traveling had I heard about something like this happening.

People would claim to meet up in dreams, but all those times it was something agreed upon ahead of time, and they were veterans in the field. But this? It was beyond crazy.

A part of me was ecstatic that she wasn't just a figment of my imagination, rationalizing that the reason why I had become so entranced by her had been because my brain recognized there was something else there. At least it made me feel less nuts over not being able to stop thinking about a delusion in my waking life.

But the more rational part of me was dying internally. My safe heaven, the only space I had ever had in my life to be with myself, had been invaded, tainted. I couldn't be alone with my thoughts anymore, someone literally had intruded on them like a parasite.

Was it even her fault?

Was this really on purpose?

"How did you get here?" I asked in the quietest, softest voice I could, trying my best not to sound accusatory and probably failing miserably.

"I don't even know where I am!" she responded, and her cries started to get louder once again. "Get me out of here!"

She started pinching herself and banging her feet against the floor, then she took her index finger and started poking at her hand with it, almost like trying to go *through it*.

I had seen that before.

"You're lucid dreaming, I think." I tried talking again, still having no idea how to prevent her from freaking out even more. "We both are."

"We're not, genius. If we were, I would be able to make this stupid **bus** actually stop!" The tears that decorated her cheeks almost seemed to mix with her freckles. "Or my stupid finger would go through my FUCKING HAND!"

She punched the seat next to her so hard her fist bounced from it.

"That's what you do?" I moved over to sit next to her, knowing that if she decided to get aggressive again she'd probably punch me instead. "*I-do-*

dhis" I said while biting my tongue.

Still nothing. My stomach dropped.

Ever since I started learning about these things, it had been my go-to reality check. It had never failed to wake me up, to make me realize I was dreaming, and I could do whatever I wanted. And that was years ago.

"You're such a masochist, why would you bite your tongue?" It was nice to have someone to talk to, but her voice wouldn't let me focus.

"I don't know, it works, ok? Give me just- Give me five minutes of silence," I pleaded, with my face on my hands and my elbows on my knees.

She rested her hand on my back, and the pressure helped, even if it was just a tiny bit.

The slow hum of the lights and the rumble of the **bus** on the pavement helped lull me into something like a meditative state. I closed my eyes and tried to let every single thought go past me, put all my worries in a neat box, and push it away. Lights, sounds, words I couldn't comprehend, everything just slid past me and kept going.

Twelve.

Memories from my high school years, back when I became obsessed with everything and anything dream related, when I learned to lucid dream for the first time. Fragments of the forums I frequented religiously, of the first times I woke up, drenched in sweat, not able to believe I had just been able to *exist* within my own mind.

Eleven

An image of the first dream journal I kept passed by, the guides I wrote down by hand because I was convinced it would help me remember them better. The hours and hours I spent waking up earlier than I should've, just so I could spend time writing down my dreams and trying to analyze them.

Ten

I saw all the times I subconsciously bit my tongue, in class and during lunch, when talking to anyone I liked. 'Just a nervous tic, ' I would say, knowing deep down I was just training myself to do so while I was sleeping too. And it had never failed me. Never ever, until now. Why now?

It was so unfair.

It didn't make sense.

No.

I had to let the thoughts go.

Nine

The air filled my lungs, and I tried to hold it for as long as I could before I exhaled. The image of a number nine filled my brain, and I slowly erased it until it was no more than a pile of chalk.

Eight

More memories of all the times I hadn't failed, of the moments where I was invincible and would just do whatever I wanted in this dreamworld I had so carefully created. All the times I was able to control this world to have superpowers, or have sex with whomever I wanted, or study longer for a test, or act out, or...

"What are you doing?" Her voice pierced through my ears.

It was okay, I could still maintain focus if I tried hard enough.

Another deep breath, more images passing through. I just observed them, never too attached to a single one to...

"Hey, you're really scaring me. Stop."

Just ignore her.

Come on.

The sounds around me were background noise. I just needed to focus on the chalkboard, on the numbers, on my breathing.

Seven.

"What's going on?!"

Well, fuck.

I opened my eyes and looked around, still on the same **bus**, still next to the same girl. Nothing had happened, nothing worked. It was a lost cause.

Her hand on my back was shaking, and her voice let me know she was going to lose it again if I didn't comply.

"I was trying to meditate," I simply responded, trying to calm her down. Now I was the one who felt defeated. "Usually when I do that, I can make myself wake up, or go deeper into the dream."

I tried really hard to put myself in her position. People expected others to open up so they could feel comfortable, and I wouldn't be able to take another fit of screaming, crying, and hitting things. I hated that I knew that. I hated having to be hyper-aware of that for my entire life.

"You sound like you have a lot of experience with these things." Her breathing was now normal, and her tears seemed to be drying up slowly. I nodded. "I've tried but never been good at it. I guess it's kind of cool."

"It's not cool, it fucks you up." The words came out of my mouth so fast I didn't really realize I had said them. She opened her mouth in shock, and I wanted to die. Again.

"It's literally dreaming, what's the worst that can happen?" She didn't sound malicious, but her words stung. "You oversleep and wake up late for work? There's way worse out there."

"You have no idea what you're talking about," I was trying to be patient and calm and all the things you're supposed to be with someone you don't know.

But holy shit, she made it so hard.

"You don't have to live with nightmares every single night," she sounded agitated, but also sad. "To be afraid of falling asleep or even closing your eyes. So yeah, I think that would be better!"

"It's not better when you get addicted to it." My voice was barely a whisper, but I knew she heard it.

"How can you—?"

"I just... I liked the control of it, and I was a teen and hormonal, and people suck. So I would just sleep and live in my dreams. I could do whatever I wanted as long as I wasn't awake. I could *be* whoever I wanted." My chest burned at that last sentence.

I wasn't talking to her anymore; I didn't care about her in that moment. All the memories that had flooded my brain kept attacking me at once. Maybe it was a nightmare, maybe I could will myself to sleep, and hopefully not remember any of this happening.

I felt pressure on my hand, and I recoiled, but she didn't let go.

"I get it," she said softly, staring at me. Like she *knew* me. "That's why I wanted to learn in the first place."

Something in that moment, in her gaze, in her hand, helped me ground. It was pointless to argue if we were both trapped together, at least until we woke up.

Something about her made her easy to talk to, like she really understood.

"I'm glad you didn't, it fucking sucked." I had forgotten how it felt to talk to someone without worrying what they would think, but why would I even care? None of this was real after all. "And now I can't get sleeping pills anymore, it's on my record or something."

Too much.

Too fucking much.

I should have bitten my tongue again.

"Why can't you—?"

"So now I come here instead!" I interrupted her, needing to move on from the topic. Putting every single one of my barriers up higher than they even were in the beginning. Smiling like I've trained my entire life. "This **bus** is a better way to ground myself first."

"Wait a minute, you're telling me you can do absolutely anything you want, and you chose... a **bus**?!"

"I... No. I mean, kind of?" I scratched my head and sighed. At least we weren't talking about me anymore. "One day I just started appearing here first, I don't know. It's like a transition before whatever comes next, the actual dream."

Explaining it out loud made it sound even crazier.

I looked down again, trying to think, and a familiar black square surprised me. My notebook, not fallen on the ground. I kneeled and picked it up, going back to sit down using the movements of the **bus**.

"What's that all about?" Her questions were getting old really quickly.

"Being alone," I turned to look at her, she gulped. "It's my alone time, that I use to write whatever I want, in peace and *quiet*."

I needed to stop being a dick.

It wasn't her fault.

But it wasn't my fault either.

"I—" She froze again, her eyes dissecting me. "I've been here. For a while. I just— I never spoke until yesterday, but I've seen you."

It was like something finally clicked on her brain, I felt shivers down my spine.

"What do you mean you've *seen* me?" I leaned back, clutching the notebook between my fingers.

"I don't know, I always take a **bus,** and you've just been there. I have no clue how this works. I thought I was awake!" She also leaned back, using her hands almost like a shield. "You're the dream expert, *you* tell me!"

The bus came to a stop before I could respond.

Finally.

I stood up, and she looked mortified.

"Sorry my dreams turned into such a nightmare for you," I said, and I really meant it. I started walking, and felt her reach out. I just needed to get down, to get this over with.

Maybe the next day would be better, two days was a coincidence, but that was it. Everything would go back to normal, I would have peace again.

"Where are you going? Don't leave me alone!" She clung to my shoulders, desperate. "I thought there were no stops, don't leave me here!"

"I have to go, calm down," I said, shaking her off me. Again, the tears, the freckles. If I stayed a minute longer, I was going to start feeling bad for her. "I told you, this just takes you to the actual dream; yours will probably come soon."

I felt guilty for leaving her like that, but she would be okay. What was the worst that could happen?

"Wait!" This time, she was the one who shouted before I exited. I could hear the fear in her voice, but it was too late to go back. "How do I know when I'm supposed to get down?"

"You'll feel it!" I screamed back, without being really sure about what that meant.

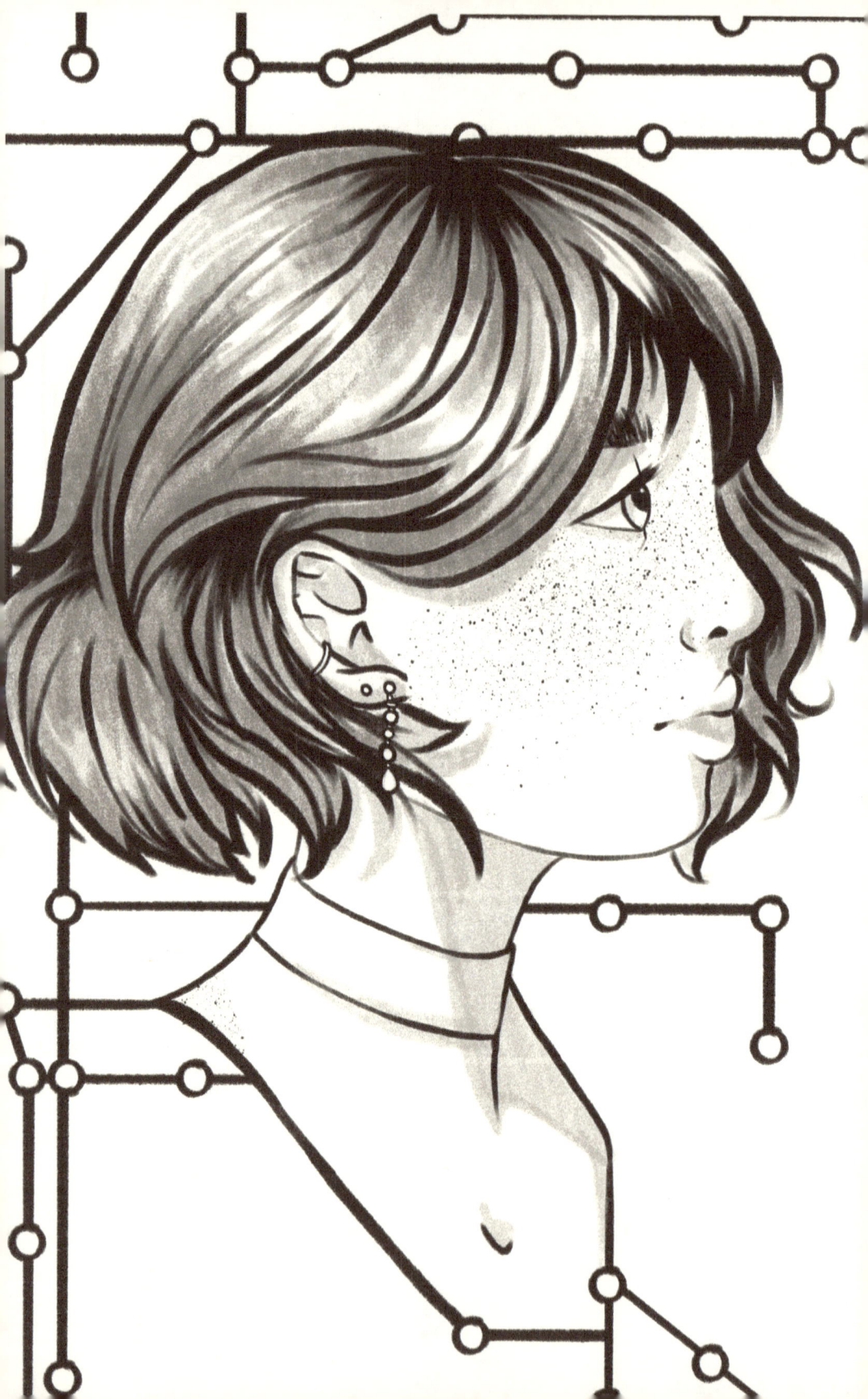

6
Curse of the Dreamer

I couldn't remember how much time had passed since the doors closed.

My muscles wouldn't react, my throat felt hoarse and raw from screaming and crying, my brain felt like giving up.

"You'll feel it," he had said. Feel what exactly?

Eventually, I just dropped myself in the same front seat he had rushed me into, too tired to move further. I waited, and waited.

Dreams.

His dreams.

Could it really be?

It felt like an eternity, and at the same time, like time wasn't passing at all. Looking around, I started to find the loops on every single person who crowded the bus.

No, not people.

Dolls.

Zombies.

A slight nod of the head, followed by a cough or an almost imperceptible balance side to side, little by little, the patterns of movement showed themselves, just a bit too precise and constant to really be *human.*

The tears on my cheeks burned less than the pain in my side, coming and going, less than the pressure on my chest.

Dreams.

A dream.

Maybe it was one, a nightmare, and I'd wake up soon enough and possibly not even remember any of that in the first place. I'd go back to ordinary life, to the *real* bus, to the *real* boy.

Unless.

Was I asleep every time I saw him?

Was he even real in the first place?

"Jasper," I tasted his name on my lips now that I knew it. Bitter. Slightly bitter. Like unsweetened tea.

"Jasper," I repeated, and could almost see the word form in smoke in front of me, dissolving as easily as my sanity was doing so in that moment.

Because I was alone in a bus that wasn't real.

With people who were not real surrounding me.

On a route that wouldn't take me anywhere.

But he felt real, more real than anything else. More real than my hair, my clothes, my boots.

He was the only thing that felt real, and he left me alone.

"Jasper!" I screamed, and I wish the bus had shaken or anyone would have been startled. Something, anything at all to show I wasn't completely irrelevant, to show that I, too, was real.

He left me alone,

but he said I would feel the stop.

He said it was his dream,

but if it was, why would I still be here?

He held me and made sure I was okay,

but he walked away afterwards.

He looked as confused as I was,

but never screamed or freaked out like I did.

He was beautiful and interesting,

but he kept pushing me away.

He saw me as I saw him,

but only because I forced him to.

He was the most interesting thing that had ever happened to me,

but part of the worst nightmare I could've ever imagined.

It felt like I was dying. The air, the monotony, they all started to feel claustrophobic. Nothing happened, nothing changed, not even the landscape outside.

Eventually, the buildings started looping too, the streetlights, the bus stops, like going in circles. Descending into a spiral with no end. My heart, my lungs, my eyes. They all felt dry and stuck, frozen. I was still able to move but, the more time passed, the more aware I was of things feeling different, weird.

Uncanny.

If it were a dream and I knew I was dreaming, I should have been able to control it. But I closed my eyes a million times, tried to will the bus to turn onto a street it hadn't before, to force one of the puppets around me to talk, something, anything. I tried, I felt the sweat mix with tears again, until my side forced me to fold over in pain.

"What was that thing I read in that one book forever ago?" I muttered to myself, desperate for any break in the silence.

Something about breathing, and a ball of energy to relax, and then counting to twelve, or was it thirteen?

But every time I closed my eyes, my pulse raced and my entire body shook. I tried again and again. One, two, three, four. One, two. One, two, three.

A loud, muffled sound.

Ringing in my ears.

I opened my eyes to see no difference in my surroundings, the same streetlights, the same fog bathing the windows. My eardrums vibrated, and yet, nothing.

That was it, I was actually going insane.

"DO SOMETHING!" The scream escaped in desperation, so loud and guttural it felt like shredding my throat into pieces.

I couldn't even recognize my own voice.

I jolted up and kneeled on the floor, trying with all my might to lift one of the seats. Then ran to the nearest stranger and stared at them for a second. Their hair was black, dull, and ugly. I punched them in the face. They didn't even bleed.

Again.

And again.

And again.

Someone else was wearing a black leather jacket. Like him.

I kicked them.

I growled, bit, hit, and pushed anyone who resembled Jasper even a little bit, every single glimmer of him. I hated him. I hated him for leaving me here. For making it seem so easy. For coming across my path in the first place. For saying my name. For calling me redhead. For not noticing me before. For leaving me here to die because the bus never stopped and the doors never opened and he left me alone to rot in a world that didn't even exist, and if it was supposed to be just a dream, why did it feel like seven years had passed but I still hadn't woken up!?

I let myself fall on the floor when I was too tired to keep it up. I curled up under a seat and just lay there with my eyes open, trying to count the swirls that decorated the rug.

One, two, three, four.

Green, pink, blue, purple.

Swirl, swirl, swirl, napkin.

And a piece of bubblegum.

Just lying there, completely oblivious to how much they stuck out.

Like me.

I kept crawling under the seats, and more things popped up, trash too specific to be part of the otherwise perfectly polished environment. Too real. Things that weren't meant to be there.

Like him.

Like me.

A jumbled receipt, a hairpin, some paper clips, an empty condom wrapping, two dimes, and a crystal.

Plus the napkin and gum.

They felt different in my hands, almost charged with electricity, like putting two magnets with the same poles together. They had this energy that felt familiar, like I had noticed before with something else.

Him.

No.

His notebook.

Trinkets left behind by others, the same way he had left his. An amulet? Something to tether him to reality?

"One day, I just started appearing here first, I don't know." He had said. "It's like a transition before whatever comes next, the actual dream."

Maybe it was not *his* dream or mine.

All the things in my hands felt like they belonged to someone at some point. Someone who, like him, had reached their stop and moved on to whatever was next.

The actual dream.

Then why wasn't I feeling my stop coming?

Maybe that was my problem; it was a dream that I was trying to make sense of, when I knew perfectly well dreams never did. I was looking for logic in the chaos. Logic, when the clock at the front of the bus was way too slow, when every time I moved someone, they went back to their position like rubber, and when the windows had survived hitting, banging, and being thrown every single thing I could find at them.

But what else was I supposed to do?

I sat down, back straight, and stared to the front. Tried not to move, not to blink, almost not to breathe. Maybe I needed to become one of them to be set free. Everything around became blurry by the second, my brain began to wander and show me flashes of memories that passed too fast for me to even realize what they were. Red, blue, green.

I was one of them, slowly melting into the seat, decomposing through the metal.

How much time had passed? Seconds? Minutes? Years?

Time felt abstract.

It *was* abstract.

We passed so many stops and I didn't react to a single one of them. The bus didn't stop. No one else came to replace him.

Heavy eyelids. Slow, slow blinking.

Blurry images of outside, of inside. Red. Blue.

Green.

Eyes weighted down by everything else around me. The rumble of the tires a strange lullaby that rippled in my ears, strangely comforting.

The world seemed more and more distant.

Blink.

Fog. Lights. Flashes. The streets floated above the clouds, grey and charged with storm. Cold, so cold. I wanted a jacket. He had a jacket. He took his jacket with him.

Blink.

Heavy eyes, heavy head, heavy breath. Bright, yellow glow coming from the windows. Non-existing traffic echoing outside, through an invisible night.

Blink

Floating, but staying in place. Couldn't breathe, couldn't move. Something, a shadow. My chest, my side, pain. Pain. Pain. Breaths, quick breaths. Paralyzed. I couldn't. Couldn't move. Everything was dark. Neon signs. Then darkness again. Darkness. Darkness. Darkness.

Blink

More shadows, all over. That loud sound I had heard before. Something was not okay. I could feel it in my skin, in my heart. Something, the time, the clock was all wrong. But I couldn't move, I couldn't speak. The things in my hand burning my skin, my bracelet growing hot. The shadows made

everything so heavy and cold and the light didn't exist outside anymore. I couldn't scream. I couldn't breathe. I could only—
Blink

Eyes. Grey eyes. Black pupils. Close, so close to me, I felt the eyelashes tickling mine. I was staring into rocks made of silver; there were no more shadows. Only warm breath that tasted like tea.

Then, he backed off.

I could move again.

"What are you doing here?" Jasper asked, more confused than upset.

He looked the same as before, without the jacket. His expression was puzzled and somewhat worried. About me?

About me.

He was worried about me!

But he left me *alone to DIE!*

"What do you mean what am I doing here?! You LIED TO ME!" I didn't really choose to jump at him, it just... happened.

He screamed, but couldn't dodge me on time. I grabbed his shirt and started shaking it. "YOU LEFT ME ALONE AND I NEVER FELT IT. THE STOP NEVER CAME!"

The button on one of my sleeves got tangled with his necklace, and his choking sounds snapped me out of it. I stopped. He was pale and even more confused than before. Shaking. Scared.

The button on one of the sleeves.

Sleeves I didn't have.

Of a jacket I was wearing now.

His jacket. He had given me his jacket.

"You were shivering," he whispered in between cries of exhaustion and fear when he saw me eyeing my wrists, his voice trembled. "I'm sorry I didn't... I didn't know, and you were shivering and... Why did you attack me? What's your problem?!"

"The bus never stopped and then I punched everyone but I couldn't break the windows and I know I took my boot off at some point. But the shadows were too much and I couldn't move and there was fog everywhere. And the clock barely moved and there was a sound and it probably has been like three minutes but you left me here. You left me and I didn't know what to do and you left—"

"It looked like you were asleep," he interrupted with a soft voice, still making sure he was putting some distance between us.

"I did, I—" I looked around. I had fallen asleep on one of the seats at the back, but was back on the front of the **bus**. "I guess I did, the shadows come when I sleep."

"The shadows?" I nodded. "Like nightmares?"

"Sleep paralysis," I whispered, staring at the floor. Too ashamed to even look at him.

At least he didn't sound upset.

"So you keep coming back, too, right? What happened during the day?" He asked, slowly inching toward me, probably realizing I didn't want to talk about the other topic.

"What do you mean during the day? I've been here." A sharp pain in my back let me know this was bad news.

"When you woke up in the morning." He spoke slowly, like he was talking to a child.

"I haven't, I guess you just woke me up right now." It was so hard to string words together.

"What do you mean you haven't woken up?" The alarm in his face was everything but comforting, he reached to grab one of my wrists, and all color drained from his face. "It's been a day already since the last time we saw each other."

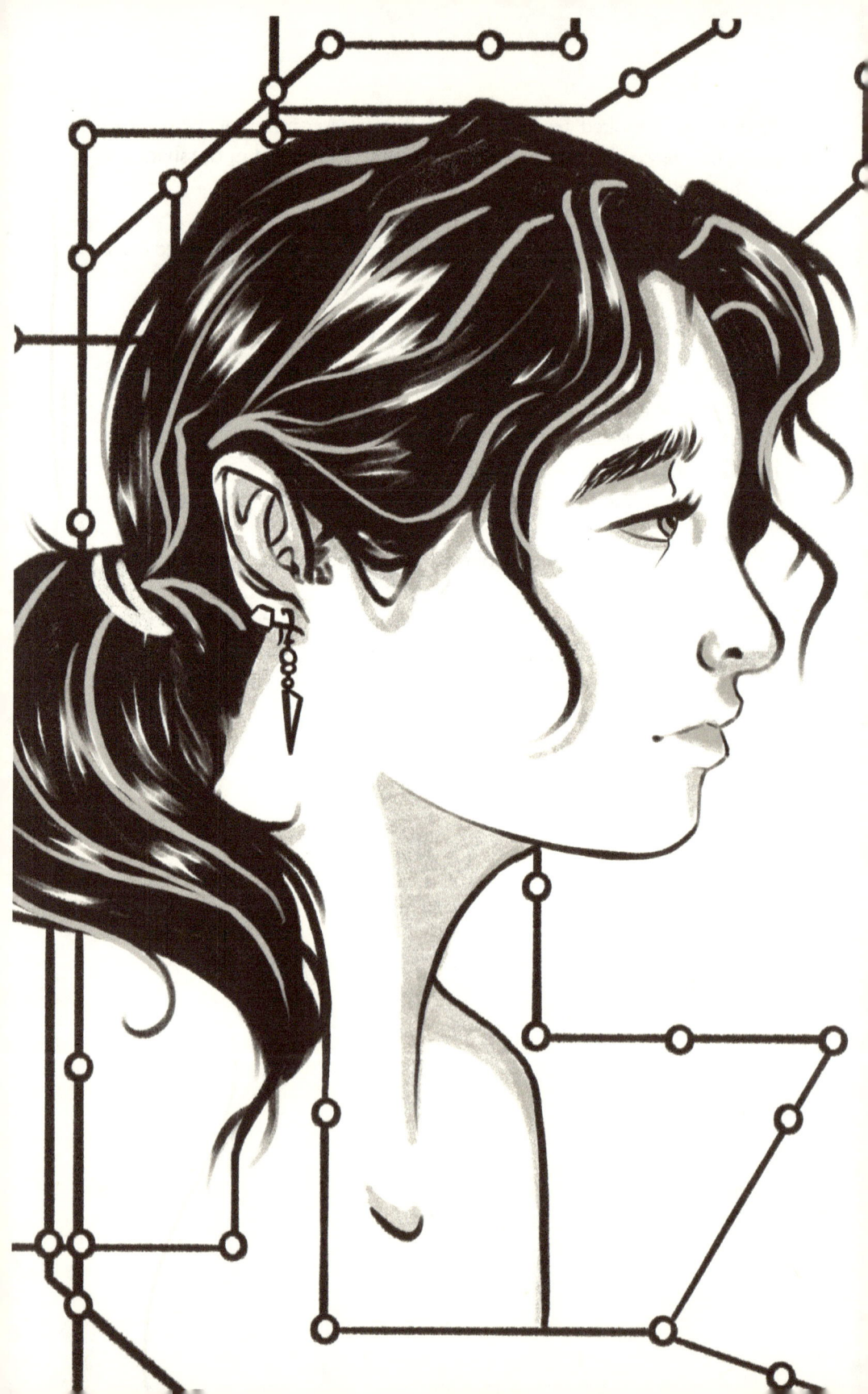

7
Jumbled Up Truths

I was fine, perfectly fine.

The twenty-seven tabs open in my work computer didn't mean anything. I was just... researching. The topic had always fascinated me; that was all.

The rest of my dreams after stepping down from the **bus** were foggy in my memory. For the first time in years, I couldn't remember them vividly, and I knew it was all because the whole situation had caught me off guard.

All because *she* had caught me off guard.

I knew it, I knew she wasn't part of my mind the second I heard her speak. There was something about her so foreign to me, to the way dreams had always worked.

So unstable and unpredictable.

Fascinating.

And that was the only reason I still had her portrait in my jacket pocket and was researching internet forums like crazy, instead of calling back the customer who had left a voice message because his laptop's camera wasn't working.

Again.

"Maybe he'll figure out the cover is probably closed and leave me alone," I muttered to myself, as if it wasn't literally my job to help him and whoever else decided to call.

Then, I realized I had spoken out loud, and my entire body jolted up in tension.

But no, thankfully, I was alone in the small office in that moment, safe from prying eyes, able to fuck around during paid time and look up if meeting other people in your dreams was actually a thing, and people on the internet weren't bullshitting everyone else after all.

It's impossible, unless your brains are connected by wires.

It's literally just a dream man

That's such bullshit

Comment after comment, I wasn't surprised in the slightest, because that's what dreams were supposed to be. Weren't they?

"Of course not, idiot. You should know better by now," my voice sounded distorted, almost like it belonged to someone else entirely.

But it was right.

I knew the theory, the magick, the chaos. I had been fucking around and finding out with reality since I was in middle school. I experienced things people would deem to be all in my head, and manifested things that would have been impossible otherwise. I had read all the books I could find, done all the exercises, spent hours meditating and visualizing, writing down notes, and trying so hard to change reality, even a little bit.

If there was a single thing I had learned from all of that, it was that intention was everything.

But *her* being there was not intentional; it was a fucking accident.

That was the piece of the puzzle that drove me insane.

The screams, the cries, the absolute pandemonium that crossed her eyes when she realized we weren't even awake told me it was impossible she had done any of that voluntarily.

But I couldn't find anything about that.

I couldn't stop thinking about it.

I couldn't breathe properly until I got home and threw myself into bed without even eating.

Until I started dreaming again.

There I was, back in the **bus,** with my notebook in hand, able to breathe. A big weight was lifted off my shoulders the second I saw the familiar windows and seats. My place, my sacred place. Alone again.

I had been worrying for nothing; it had been a one-off, weird incident that would never happen again. Or I was delusional, and it had actually just been a dream, and this whole obsession had been so fucking stupid, and it just showed how pathetic I...

There she was.

Sitting all the way in one of the front seats- still, too still. I walked towards her without even wanting to believe it was happening again, not sure if I was upset my sanctuary had been intruded upon a third time or grateful I was seeing her one more time. I came as close as I could, probably closer than I should have.

Still? No.

Trembling. Shivering.

Like we were outside during the winter.

"Chiara?" I whispered, but she didn't respond.

Her eyelids were closed, but I could see her eyeballs moving underneath them at unnerving speeds. I took my jacket off without thinking about it too much and grabbed her wrist.

Still shivering, still unresponsive.

One arm, then the second one. Her lashes fluttered above her freckles. I came even closer to her face because a part of me got the idiotic thought that maybe she wasn't breathing, when I felt a warm exhalation. And then, her eyes opened violently.

"What are you doing here?" I couldn't help but ask and immediately regretted it.

Her expression changed from confusion to happiness, to fear, to anger.

"What do you mean what am I doing here?!" Her voice scratched the inside of my ears like a nail. "You LIED TO ME!"

She fucking jumped at me like an insane, rabid animal that hadn't seen any other living being in at least several months. I screamed and tried to dodge her, but she was too fast and too fucking strong, and two seconds later, she was screaming in my face, and I needed to get out of there before I did something I would regret even more.

I tried to shake her off and then felt something yanking around my neck, choking me.

She was killing me. This crazy, feral girl was trying to actually kill me inside my own dream, and I was too stupid to defend myself because I had gotten too close too fast and now she was choking me and I was probably going to die in real life and...

She let go, untangling the button of my own jacket with the silver necklace I forgot I was wearing.

No choking, still alive.

She looked at the jacket like it was an alien artifact; she hadn't even noticed.

"You were shivering!" I tried to scream, but my voice sounded like cracked whispers. Maybe if I explained I was actually trying to be nice and help, she would stop trying to attack me. I didn't want to die anymore, damn, at least not at that moment. "I'm sorry I didn't... I didn't know, and you were shivering and... Why did you attack me? What's your problem?!"

I sounded pathetic.

I should've pretended she didn't exist.

Her mouth kept saying things, but I couldn't focus. The world kept twisting and turning around me, and I needed to think, and couldn't do it with her constantly blabbering on and on about punching people and breaking windows and... fog? Clocks?

"It looked like you were asleep," I stayed with the topic of the jacket, in an attempt to excuse myself for having put it on her without her consent. I shouldn't have, that was stupid and honestly kind of disrespectful too, and...

Did she mention shadows when she sleeps?

"The shadows?" I asked, looking around. "Like, nightmares?"

"Sleep paralysis," she responded, looking so uncomfortable, I couldn't bear to pry more.

Sleep paralysis.
Shadows.
Nightmares inside a dream.

She was different, like I suspected. Everything around her challenged every single notion of reality and dream I ever had. Did she even realize that? Was her waking life affected by this as much as mine was?

"So you keep coming back, too, right? What happened during the day?" I asked and moved closer, trying to appear as least threatening as possible. Too intrigued to listen to my gut screaming for me to back the fuck up again.

"What do you mean during the day? I've been here."

Talking to her was as hard as trying to make a child comprehend why they couldn't have candy for breakfast, lunch, and dinner.

"When you woke up in the morning." I grabbed my temples and exhaled. I had to keep my composure, but it was proving to be extremely hard.

"I haven't, I guess you just woke me up right now." She was dragging her words a little, like she was still recovering after the burst from seconds ago.

Or minutes?

How much time had passed?

I took a glance at the clock and nodded.

Minutes, good, at least that's working fine.

But something else was broken; it took me a moment to fully register what she had said. I felt all the blood draining from my face, and now I was the one shivering.

"What do you mean you haven't woken up?" Something was wrong, very wrong. "It's been a day already since the last time we saw each other."

"No, it wasn't." The certainty with which she said it made me shiver.

"How did you get back to the bus after you left it, then?" Someone able to come and go in between dreams? That was more than extraordinary.

"I didn't, because you lied to me!" She started to raise her voice again, but caught herself. "You told me I would feel it, that the doors would open for me!"

It sounded like a plea. The feral creature she had been before now seemed wounded and scared.

"I tried everything, and then the punching, and eventually went under the seats and found all this trash," she started taking things out of her pocket. A receipt, a crystal, some other trash, and... was that a fucking condom wrapper?!

I visibly recoiled, but she didn't even seem to notice, too entranced staring at the random things in her hands to even realize anything else.

"What's all of that about?" I couldn't help but furrow my brows and back up a little bit. It was happening; she was absolutely losing her mind.

"They feel like... your notebook," she simply said, dragging her words again.

Maybe she had already lost her mind.

"They what?!" I said, and instinctively grabbed the notebook I had left a few seats away and held it next to my chest.

It had appeared in my hands as soon as I opened my eyes and was in that **bus**, as usual. My small anchor to myself, to my thoughts, to my world.

"Your notebook feels like... electric? Magnetic?" She started trying to explain, and when she extended her hand to try to touch it, I almost let her. Almost. "When you left it here, I kept it, but it was weird, and it only had scribbles, but it felt weird in my hands, like this." She came forward and put a paperclip in my empty hand.

It *did* feel different.

"I think these are like that for you, things from other people that left the **bus** and never came back."

The silence after her words was heavy. Sticky.

Things didn't make sense in dreams; that was the whole point, and yet that sounded so logical. If I was there, and she was there, how many other people would have been there before us?

But why us? Why now?

Why had I never seen another conscious soul in all the time I had spent using the **bus**?

I wished I had more time, I wished she knew more, I wished I had been more prepared. All the doomscrolling during the day had left me empty-handed and empty-headed, all a fucking waste of time. It had to mean something; it had to have a reason.

Why did we keep meeting each other like that?

Why couldn't I get her out of my head?

Why didn't she wake up?

Why was she breathing so heavily?

Her chest moved violently, and my mouth went dry almost at the same time the **bus** started slowing down.

Fuck, I felt it. That tingling sensation all over my skin. Again. It was too late.

"No..." she whispered, and froze on the spot.

I couldn't do it, I couldn't leave her there knowing that something was clearly wrong.

'You LIED TO ME!' She had said, but how was I supposed to know the **bus** wasn't going to stop for her?

I reached out and grabbed her hand without a second thought. She tensed, but didn't seem to want to let go.

"I'm sorry I left you alone," I said, without being able to look her in the eye. "I won't make the same mistake twice."

"Where are we going?" Her voice was barely audible, and her hand was sweating.

The bus stopped with a sudden jerk, and I moved to the door before my worries caught up to me and convinced me to leave without her. She followed me like a shadow, almost as desperate as I felt in that moment.

"I think I'm taking you to my dreams," I responded without fully understanding what that meant.

Then, I stepped out.

Then, her hand slipped off mine.

I turned around and saw her looking at the asphalt inches away from her feet, pale and shaking. Mortified.

"Are you coming?" I sounded impatient; maybe a part of me was. But the other part didn't seem to want to let the mystery go, the stubborn and obsessive part.

The same part of me that had kept her portrait and convinced the rest of me to grab her hand.

"It's so high," she whispered, her voice shaking with fear. "I'm going to fall and die. It's too high. I can't. I can't jump."

"It's just a step," I came closer, the doors tried to close on her, and she screeched.

"It's too high, Jasper, I'm gonna die. I'm gonna die. I'm gonna die!" Tears once again decorated her face. Screams escaping desperately from her throat.

Clank

The bus doors tried to close on her body again, pushing her inwards. She grabbed them to stabilize herself.

Clank

"Chiara, just jump. Okay? Just. Just do it!" What the fuck was I supposed to do?

For the first time, the passengers inside the **bus** started to move. To speak.

"Close the door!"

"Get inside!"

"Start the bus!"

They were nagging, complaining, almost like real people.

Almost.

Clank

One of them pulled her shirt from behind and she almost fell backwards. She screamed and pushed forward, but couldn't get herself to jump. Something was trying to keep her inside at all costs.

Clank

I jolted forward and wrapped her waist with my arms, wrestling her from the grip of the almost perfect copies of something that could have been human.

She cried.

We fell back.

The doors finally closed, and the bus was gone in an instant.

We stayed there for a second, shaking on the fake sidewalk.

Locked in an embrace I didn't even realize I had been needing for a very long time.

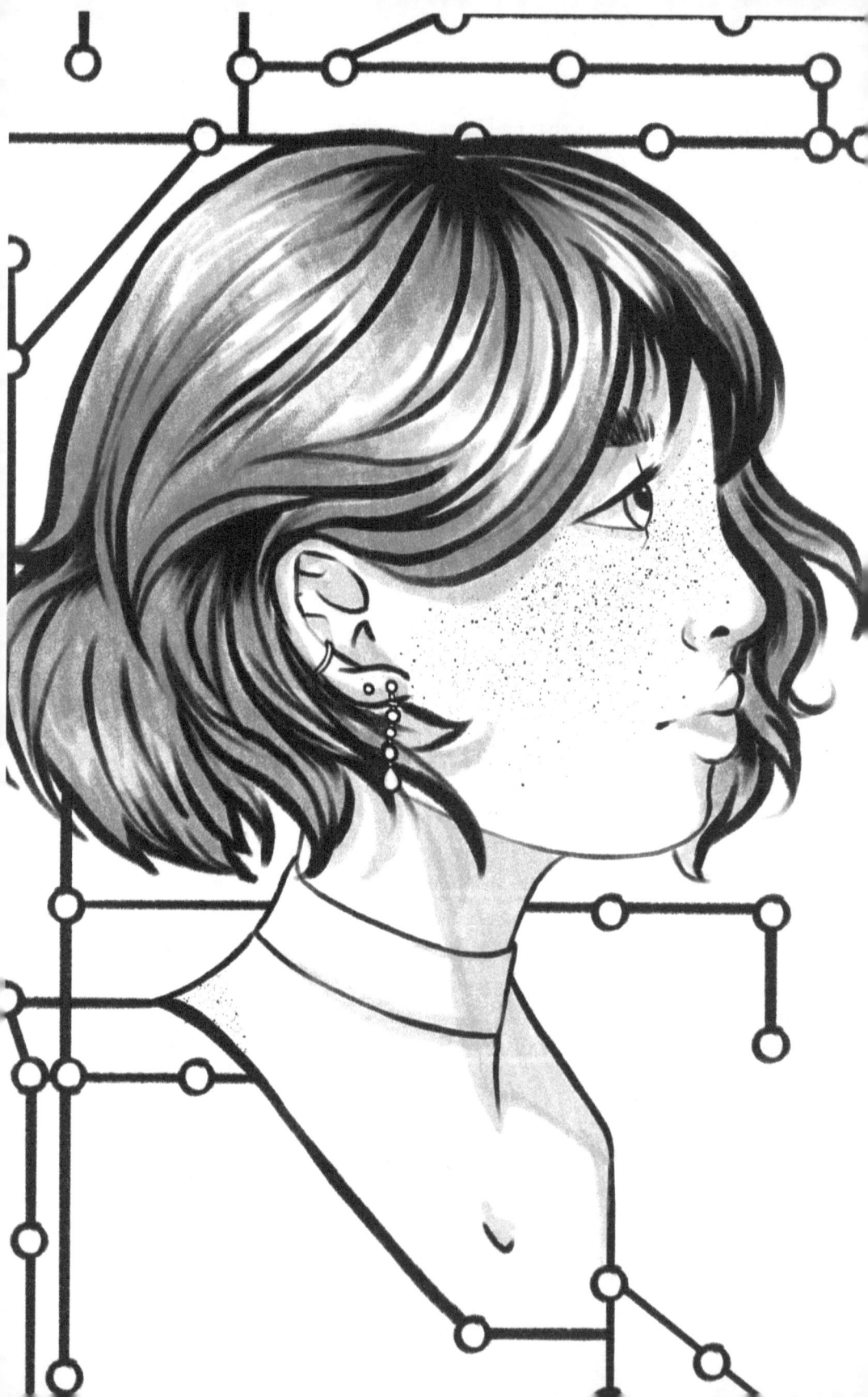

8
Challenging the Illusion

I was going to die.

At any moment, I would fall and plunge to my death.

That's it, the end of me as I knew it. Maybe it was for the best, maybe that's what this was all about. A liminal space, a purgatory taking me to the underworld.

The **bus** was the boat, and the void under me was the river Styx.

A river of pure white mist, stretching down to a bottomless abyss.

I tried to look for Jasper with my sight, but only a blur remained where his silhouette had been a second ago. Nothing past the **bus** felt tangible anymore. His voice came to me from a place far, far away, behind me, ahead of me, surrounding me.

"It's too high, Jasper, I'm gonna die. I'm gonna die. I'm gonna die!" I couldn't see clearly, I couldn't breathe. My eyes were inundated by rivers of salt, my throat hoarse from the pain of certain death looming under my feet.

The pain of something hitting my sides. One time. Two times.

The doors started trying to cut me in half, pushing and pulling and begging to rip my skin. Trying desperately to push me inside. But no, I couldn't go back to the madness of boredom and uncertainty, of being trapped within that metal prison.

I couldn't.

I couldn't.

I couldn't.

I wouldn't.

I held onto the same doors, trying to trap myself or send me to the abyss, and stabilized myself as much as I could.

"Chiara, just jump. Okay? Just. Just do it!"

Did he want me to die? Was this all a ploy?

I shook my head to get rid of the thick tears blurring my vision, to no avail. I couldn't move. I couldn't breathe. The pain, the pain in my sides.

The pain in my back.

The pushing.
The pulling.
Hands behind me, grabbing onto my clothes, onto my hair.
"Close the door!"
I screamed again. Weren't we alone?
"Get inside!"

The same people who were not people, the ones I had tried so desperately to force to act in any way that could resemble a human. They were here to get their revenge.

"Start the bus!"

'No!' My mind tried to project, but the word never left my mouth. I couldn't go back, I couldn't jump, I couldn't move.

A hand wrapped around my ankle, a foot kicked the back of my knee. They complained and screamed at the driver, but their words felt like an echo of something that had never been alive, crawling in my ears like caterpillars escaped from a place they didn't belong in the first place.

The pain, again. The doors still threatening my sides.

Even if I tried to jump, I couldn't anymore. My muscles wouldn't react and the pain in my ribs was so strong I was folding in half. They were pulling me, taking me, and I wasn't even able to fight it anymore.

Would I be stuck in that boat forever? Wouldn't it be better if I could just jump to the river of souls?

Why was this even happening?

What was it with that cursed **bus** that was so committed to destroying my psyche?!

More hands, arms wrapped around me so strongly, maybe that was how I would end up breaking in half. But this time, they came from the front.

My eyes were open, but I still couldn't see; the whiteness devoured it all.

But the smell, that bitter, unsweetened tea.

It was him.

His arms.

His hair.

His face, right next to mine.

I let the doors go and cried.

He fell back, and I fell into his arms.

Reality was slowing down, the world stopped spinning, and the colors were coming back.

His smell, his warmth, they reminded me I was still alive. Alive and there, with him, the boy I adored since way before he knew I even existed. He had saved me; he was holding me like he knew how much it meant.

Like he knew we were connected somehow.

I closed my eyes and let myself be there for a split second, until his face blurred and I forgot what it looked like, until the only thing that was left was how he made me feel in that moment.

Because that was all that mattered in the end. Right?

The feeling, the idea, the mystery, the chase. The fluttering of butterflies in my entrails whenever he was close, the daydreaming and wondering. The yearning.

He hadn't been the first, probably wouldn't be the last.

At least it felt right in that moment; it was enough to give me what I needed, without it being too much.

I had to treasure it, know I couldn't ruin it by opening my mouth or asking too many questions or getting too close too fast or—

"Are you okay?" He whispered in my ear, and I forgot my name. My entire body shivered in goosebumps.

I opened my eyes and saw his, so close to mine.

His irises, surrounded by white so similar to the one that threatened to drown me moments ago, hours ago.

Time didn't exist anymore.

"Sanpaku eyes." The words leaving my mouth felt foreign. "The Japanese think people with eyes like yours have a life with constant misfortune."

What the hell was wrong with me?!

"They might be right," he responded, furrowing his brow. Then, he smiled. "But not today."

The spell was broken, and we separated, stood up, and went back to our own worlds.

I wrapped my arms around myself even though I wasn't even cold anymore; his jacket still covered me like a security blanket, and I knew I should give it back.

But it was his.

And now I had it.

He had given it to me.

I turned to look at him, and he seemed confused, looking around, searching for something that wasn't there. His expression looked crumpled, anguished.

We were standing on a sidewalk in the middle of nowhere, sure.

But the sky was a stunning royal blue, with an array of twinkling stars that seemed to be shining brighter than usual. Some silver, like the strands decorating his hair. Some yellow, like the bracelets I wore.

The emptiness was vast, but not suffocating like the abyss from before. It tasted like possibility and running in any direction; it smelled like freedom.

It looked like a gas station with neon lights, almost begging us to go.

Like a mirage in the desert.

But what if it was an oasis?

"What's that?" I pointed at it; he shuddered with surprise and turned to look where I was pointing.

His confusion became more palpable.

"I... I don't know." He extended the words, like he was afraid of saying them. "I don't know, I really don't—"

"I thought you said this was your dream?" I answered, almost in an apology. He seemed almost devastated.

"I'm not sure, I've never seen this place. I felt the stop coming, and the bus stopped, so I thought. Fuck. I really thought— but I don't—" He walked towards the bus stop next to us and checked behind it, as if the answers were there. "Maybe it's yours?"

"Probably not, I didn't feel anything other than almost dying back there," I said and shook the memories away. "Anyway, let's check it out!"

I started walking, and he immediately jolted forward.

I couldn't stay there. What if the **bus** came back? What if it tried to eat me? To trap me?

The sky was so pretty and full of wonder, it finally felt like a dream, like magic surrounding us. My footsteps were light, like gravity had started to take time as an example and was distorting as well. The neon lights sizzled in the distance, and seemed so far, but so close, and far again.

"What are you doing?" I heard his footsteps before I saw him pop next to me, and my chest felt warm.

He was following me.

He wanted to be with me.

"Getting as far away from that bus stop as I can," I said, pointing back. I wasn't going to be trapped again. "If you want to stay and wait for the **bus** to come back, be my guest."

'Please say no.'

'Please say no.'

'Please say no.'

'Please say no.'

'Please say no.'

'Please say no.'

"What? No! I told you I wasn't going to leave you alone again!"

'Oh, thank goodness,' I thought to myself, but just smiled.

We walked in silence for a while. Me, hugging his jacket and trying to sneak as many stares as I could, trying to get as close as I could without directly bumping into him. Him, probably lost in his own thoughts, with his hands in his pockets and his eyes anywhere but me.

I wanted to talk about something, anything to keep my own thoughts at bay. Whatever had happened when I tried to leave —when I clearly almost died— still lingered in my brain in a way that was starting to eat me alive.

But I tried to be nonchalant, to walk with my back straight and have a smile that seemed natural, just in case he looked in my direction.

It was stupid, I knew that.

He didn't really care about me. He had left me alone once. He was just being polite. He was stuck with me.

"Are you okay?" His voice broke the silence, sending me into a coughing fit. "Shit, are you—"

"Yes! Fine. Thanks." I responded in between coughs and put a hand on my chest to stabilize myself. It felt hot and raspy, my side started aching again.

"You said you were gonna die back there." That wasn't even a question, and yet it seemed like he was waiting for a response.

"What did you see?" I asked instead, starting to walk once again, wrapping myself with my arms.

"You standing at the doors, nothing weird really."

"I saw white." I paused, surprised I was saying it out loud. "A white abyss. Tall, like a cliff, but with nothing at the bottom. I couldn't see you, I could barely hear you."

I got upset at the tears in my eyes, but let them fall, drying them off would have made them too obvious.

"And the pain on my sides. It was like the doors were going to cut me in half." My voice cracked. "I don't know, this whole thing is just so weird."

He nodded in silence, but didn't say anything else. We kept walking until the lights bathed us and the neon became a low hum, background noise.

Then, music.

Glorious.

A mix of beats that sounded like the remnants of things I would listen to when I was younger. Lyrics that were almost words, melodies that made me feel almost home.

I ran inside, and the music grew louder. A smile tugged at the corners of my mouth; it was bright and beautiful and warm.

"Hello?" I heard from behind me as Jasper entered.

I turned to see him, cautious, calm, with a customer service smile that didn't really reach his eyes. His gaze bounced from one corner to the other, like trying to absorb as much information as possible, like he was making a mental map of the place.

Hadn't he been nervous right before? Worried?

It was like a switch had flipped in his brain.

"Hello?" he asked again, with a deeper than usual voice, standing a little bit too straight.

When no one responded, he went back to his more relaxed position.

Relief washed over me when no weird zombies came by, no one who would move like rubber if I tried to shake their hand or pull their arm.

We were alone, surrounded by colors and the breeze of what was probably the idea of an AC and the mix of the night's breeze. Surrounded by cans and bags of candy and—

"Oh my God, remember this?!" I screamed, running towards the can of my favorite soda when I was a kid. "They discontinued it like a decade ago!"

He chuckled. Was that the first time I saw him smile?

He stood there for a second and took a deep breath. *"X-treeeeeem!"* He mocked the commercials while pretending to snowboard.

So he had a sense of humor after all; there was something else besides the brooding, mysterious vibe he surrounded himself with. I laughed, and it seemed to relax him more; for a second, he had a placid smile on his face.

I put my nail under the cap of the can and felt his hand wrap around my wrist the second I heard it hiss as it opened.

"Are you sure that's a good idea?" He seemed concerned again, looking in all directions.

"Why wouldn't it be?" I looked around as well, trying to make sure I hadn't missed anything.

Were there zombies after all? Weird humanoids trying to get us? Were they going to drag us back to the **bus**?

Nothing.

Just the music, and the lights, and the colors, and the night.

"What if it's like... the fae realm?" He whispered and looked at the ground, like he was ashamed of even mentioning it. He started fiddling with his fingers, the chips on the sides of his black nails telling me it was probably more frequent than he would have admitted.

But it made sense.

"Isn't the point of it, that if you eat something from the fae, you can't go back?" I asked. He nodded in relief. I nodded back and took a sip. "Perfect."

I took another sip.

I didn't have anyone to get back to anyway.

9
Joining Forces

"What if it's like... the fae realm?"

I knew I was going to say something stupid before I opened my mouth, and did it anyway.

I looked down to try to calm myself. What would she think about me? Would she just assume I'm some crazy woo-woo dude that believes in way too many things he can't prove?

Wouldn't she be right?

Why do I care anyway?

"Isn't the point of it, that if you eat something from the fae, you can't go back?" She responded, and I looked up to catch the glimpse in her eyes.

She understood.

Then, she took a sip.

"Perfect!" she said, taking another one.

Fuck.

"No!" I couldn't stop myself. I tugged at her wrist, and the soda spilled all around us.

"I was joking!" she let out a laugh that didn't quite meet her eyes. Still dark, emptiness behind the sparkles the light reflected on them.

She wasn't, we both knew it.

"What if now you can't wake up for real?" I asked and then realized I was still holding her, maybe with way more pressure I should have used. "We don't know what's going on, what's going to make this worse." I backed off so fast the shelf behind me almost fell over.

We stood there, looking at each other for what felt like hours, but the clock on the back wall kept reminding me it was just seconds. It's like the weight of the idea was crushing both of us slowly.

I couldn't bear it anymore, so I picked up the can that had fallen to the floor and walked to the counter to throw it away.

"I don't want to go back to a world where I can't taste this, and the stars don't shine like those outside," she whispered, and every single bone in my body wanted to turn around to look at her. I just couldn't.

Another fizz, another gulp.

We were already fucked anyway.

That feeling was too real.

Too painful.

I wouldn't want to go back either.

More minutes passed, and I heard her moving, slowly walking through the shelves while I stood frozen in place, looking at everything but her.

Was this place really isolated?

Why had the bus stopped there?

Where did my dreams go?

Why couldn't I look at her?

What was I so afraid of?

Finally, when I heard her come closer to me, I turned around.

"Do you like coconut?" She had a smile on her face again, a soda in one hand, and some snack in the other. "I found this, and something told me you'd like it."

It was a long brown package with a palm tree. Layers of wafer with coconut cream in between, kisses decorating the glossy paper. My jaw almost fell to the floor.

"Where was this?" I said, almost gasping for air.

"Right over there." She pointed to where the fridges were. "So... you like it? Are you not mad at me anymore?" Her tone was absurdly playful, almost rehearsed, almost worried.

I almost ripped the package out of her hands, opened it with strength that wasn't really needed, and took a bite that tasted like glory.

Fuck the fae realm. Fuck the idea of waking up again.

It was fucking unbelievable. It tasted exactly like I remembered.

"Cocosette," I said with my mouth full. "Venezuelan. So good. My mom would get me these all the time when I was a kid."

"But you don't have an accent," she said, and I could see the regret immediately wash over her face. "I mean—"

"Who said I have to have one to be foreign?" I responded with a smile and couldn't help but chuckle.

"No, no, like, you don't *have* to, I just— I wasn't expecting— You don't look like—" The desperation in her pitch was adorable.

'I have to stop thinking about her that way,' my brain reminded me. I brushed it off for just a second.

"I was little when we moved," I responded with a shrug that would hopefully let her know it was okay.

"I'm so sorry, that was so wrong." Ironically, her nervousness calmed me down. It made everything feel less threatening. "Here, let me get you something else."

"Chiara, you don't have to—" I started, but she had already ran off to the fridges.

I walked up to her with a smile on my face and managed to only look around in case some unexpected danger would jump at us from behind a corner like, three times.

Only three times.

Impressive.

"You already ate something, so the fae have us both," she played, while opening the fridge door and trying to reach for the back.

"What are you doing?" It was as if she was trying to get swallowed by all the beer cans.

"Everybody knows the best ones are always in the back," she responded, so casually.

Like we weren't stuck in a dream either of us knew who it belonged to. Like she didn't feel like she was dying about an hour ago. Like she had forgotten about the panic attacks and being trapped in that **bus**, with those fake people.

Like she was unstoppable.

For a second, I wished I—

A screech came out of her mouth as she tripped and slid one of the shelves to the back.

Then another one followed, and another one.

The cans melted slowly towards the floor, and she jumped back as we stood there, watching as they disappeared through cracks that didn't exist a second ago.

And the back wall of the fridge opened up with a creak.

And a musty basement appeared in front of our eyes.

"Well, fuck," I whispered, feeling my lungs about to come out of my throat.

"That looks like a sign to me," she said with that smile still on, and grabbed my hand. My cold, clammy hand. "Maybe there are some answers there!"

"This looks absolutely fucking dangerous."

But I let myself be dragged in- what was the alternative anyways?

So there we were, in a cold, dusty basement that smelled like mold.

Dark, filled with furniture covered by cloth and an enormous pool table in the middle. The walls were decorated with cracks that looked like vines, the ceiling with malfunctioning tiny bulbs that almost looked like dying stars.

Chiara started inspecting everything with such calm, so sure of herself. She pulled the cloth and touched the rotting wood, tried to jump to touch the bulbs, jumped up to the pool table.

I wished I were that confident.

"Jasper, I really think we're the only ones here." She cocked her head to one side, like she was trying to listen to something nonexistent.

"But you were the one who found the trinkets, you were the one who said more people have been there," I didn't want to raise my voice; it just... happened. "How can you be so calm knowing that everything could go wrong so quickly?!"

"I meant here, in this place, basement thing." She furrowed her brow and shrank a little into herself. Of course, I would make her uncomfortable. I needed to stop being an asshole. "You're the one that's been jumping in and out of dreams, I don't know, shouldn't you be the calm one?!"

"I've been in *my* dreams." I started emphasizing with my hands. "Where *I* can set *my* rules." My voice was trembling now, my hands shaking. "Where *I* am in *control!*"

Something broke in my throat at that last word. Fear stole the last sound. It left me slumped on the pool table next to her.

She stayed quiet, gave me time to breathe, caressed my hair with her fingers.

"I'm afraid too," she whispered when my breath returned to a more regular pace. "That's why I keep moving."

At least she didn't hate me, at least she didn't think I was overreacting.

I mean, she's the one who's gone screaming and crying.

Maybe we're not so different after all.

I sat next to her, our knees touched the tiniest bit. She didn't move away. I smiled.

The felt on the table was a shade of blue I didn't recognize, like the reflection of the moon in an ocean filled with luminous algae. The balls shone like small fish trying to get away from us, rolling slowly away and bouncing against the borders. Red, yellow, green, black.

That black ball, trying to get away faster than all the other ones.

Wouldn't it be funny if—?

I leaned to grab it; it tried to flush itself into one of the corners, but I caught it in time. The number eight on it pulsated.

Maybe it wasn't that bad to let go of control for a little while, to welcome the unexpected. Maybe she was right and as long as we kept moving, the bad stuff wouldn't be able to get to us.

As long as we kept moving.

"Is this somebody else's dream?" I asked the ball, and Chiara stiffened for a second, then she leaned forward to see.

I waited, almost holding my breath.

The eight kept pulsating, the ball started to warm up.

She waited, probably holding her breath too. One of her hands found its place to my knee, to steady herself.

We waited, but the ball grew cold. I turned it around, trying to find any secret, any magical window, any answer hidden inside its—

"Oh wow," Chiara's voice interrupted my thoughts. Each time, it bothered me less and less. "Check it out!"

The felt became liquid and the rest of the balls dissolved on it like cotton candy. Slowly, words appeared on the surface, like drawn with shadows.

'Cannot predict now'

"Bruh."

Chiara started laughing the second the word left my mouth, almost hysterically. I laughed with her, how could I not?

The words dissipated. An empty space, ready for the next plea.

"My turn!" She announced, taking the ball from my hands. "Why are we here? Together?" Her words came out in a whisper, her eyes stayed where the answer was meant to be.

Not for a second did she look away.

Not even when her cheeks flushed and her nose turned red.

I let myself smile; at least she didn't realize my cheeks looked the same.

"Better not to... tell you now?" She read aloud in a confused tone. "What does that even mean?"

A loud thump coming from the wall that the basement shared with the gas station took the question away. The table started melting into the floor. Slowly.

She opened her mouth to scream, but thankfully the years of paranoia and hyper vigilance finally came to use. I put my hands on her mouth with more strength than I needed to. We both fell back and to the floor.

Another thump, closer to the door.

Fuck. Fuck. Fuck. Fuck.

I knew it.

I fucking knew something was wrong.

I shouldn't have let my guard down.

I shouldn't have listened to her.

Thump. Thump. Thump.

The lights went off.

This time, we both screamed.

A loud crash and sounds of broken glass put me on my knees again, and I got up with shaking legs and intense nausea. I helped her get up as well, illuminated by a single, electric blue light that buzzed on top of stairs that had been hidden by shadows before.

It was too perfect, too convenient.

A trap. It had to be a trap.

Chiara was already halfway to the top.

Silence.

She opened her mouth to say something and stopped.

Not a single sound.

Not even the buzz from the light.

Not from behind us.

Not from the room.

The dark became darker, the shadows in Chiara's face elongated it, made her look skinnier, grey.

She had stopped in the middle of the stairs. Waiting for me.

Something slithered close to my back, without touching it.

Enough to make the hair on my neck raise.

Still in silence, a thin cable started floating towards her.

No.

Not again.

The same fucking bullshit that happened at the **bus.**

Fuck me.

"Run!" I yelled.

I did so.

She didn't move.

I ran past her and grabbed her by her waist. The silence was broken by the intense moans of a machine, electricity. Cables came out of the walls and started climbing at our feet.

"I can't. I can't. I can't. I can't. I can't." She was stiff; it was so hard to drag her up the final couple of steps. "I can't move. Jasper. Jasper, I can't. I can't move."

Like at the fucking bus.

"I'm sorry, Jasper. I'm so sorry." I could feel her desperation. "It's my fault. I asked the question. I said there was no one here. It's me. It wants me. It hates me!"

We arrived at the door and I grabbed her with one hand while trying to turn the knob with the other.

"Listen to me, Chiara, I won't let anything happen to you. Okay?" I was screaming just to quiet the static sounds around us. "I don't give a fuck whose fault it is. We're in this together."

But, were we?

I kept telling myself that I could run, just leave her there.

I could've left her on the bus, too.

But I couldn't, I wouldn't.

The door opened, and I pushed both of us through it.

It closed behind us with a heavier sound than it should've made. Something locked it from the outside, like a safe.

But no cables wrapped around our ankles nor the sounds of static attacked us.

Chiara sat on the floor, finally able to move again, checking something in her legs. I leaned down to see rope burns where her fishnet stockings showed skin. There were probably more hidden underneath her boots.

She looked in pain.

I felt... fine.

My legs were tired, but that was it. It seemed like the cables hadn't done as much damage to me.

But had I *actually* felt the cables around my ankles?

I was wearing pants, sure, but it surely had to have hurt me even a little.

Maybe she was right.

I rolled my pants leg up. Not a single bruise.

Fuck. It wants her.

Only her.

"We should keep going," I said, stumbling over the words as if it were the first time I had ever said them.

It took Chiara a couple of seconds to react, to realize that there was something else in existence other than just the scratches on her legs. The redhead just looked up and turned to me.

"Where? You saw what happened when we started poking into what we shouldn't have," she replied with tears in her eyes. "For listening to me."

She looked down again, and something inside me broke. Suddenly, it occurred to me that I would much rather face a horde of zombies with thousands of cables scratching my legs than see more tears in those eyes.

Those deep, green eyes.

Fuck.

I couldn't focus, I— I couldn't let my feelings win.

Not then and there.

What feelings, anyway?

I had to think straight.

I didn't even know this girl to begin with.

Quiet.

Panic started accumulating in my chest, and yet, still silence on the other side of the door.

And on our side?

A musty hallway with doors on both sides. The walls were a combination of wood and stone, fusing together, battling to decide which material won.

I walked toward her and wrapped my arms around her shoulders. My jacket was now history, probably in the clutches of the mechanical monster that was stalking us.

No.

That was stalking *her*.

"Maybe there's a light at the end of this tunnel?" I tried to make a joke, pointing to what seemed to be an infinite hallway.

And then, I heard what I had said.

And wanted to die.

"Oh God, Jasper, don't say that!" She pretended to be offended, but at least chuckled. "That thing hasn't killed us *yet.*"

I made her chuckle.

I made her chuckle!

And now, her eyes weren't filled with tears.

Now, she was using my hands to steady herself and stand up. Now, she was walking next to me, and at least the cries had stopped.

I did that!

We walked and walked, our feet pounding the ground with each step. The hallway turned, and turned again. It became a mess of doors that flickered in neon flashes and disappeared, or changed location as soon as we got close to them.

Some of them were made of wood, others of metal. Some looked like tinted glass. Some seemed to be almost liquid.

The metal ones were the worst.

Every single time we walked past one of them, I had to look away.

Something wasn't right,

something in her reflection.

She didn't seem to notice, just kept walking. And walking. And walking.

"Do you think eventually one of them would open?" She asked after almost every single time she tried one.

We kept walking. And walking.

And walking.

Until the seconds turned into hours.

And her reflection kept acting up.

It kept showing me things.

Blood.

There were no sounds, no persecution, no monsters coming to get us.

I counted seventy-six doors. Seventy-seven. None of them opened.

I avoided the metal ones.

She didn't.

They remained closed.

I tried to stare at it a few times, whatever distorted view the metal ones tried to give me of her. Something started screaming at me inside my head each time, begging me to look away.

Blood.

Something kept screaming. It kept repeating something again and again until it was drumming my ears so loudly I had to cover them with both of my hands. It didn't stop, the screams were coming from the inside.

Time is running out.

"Did you hear me?" She was staring at me with her lips pursed and her head cocked. It took me a second to realize she had spoken. "Jasper?"

"I'm sorry, what?" My head was spinning. At least she didn't have blood on her. The reflections had to be lying.

My hands trembled.

"Do you think it's true?" She asked, like it was the third time. I looked at her, confused. "The thing. The thing about other people being in our place from before! You know, the whole deal with the trinkets and stuff? That maybe this already happened to someone else..."

She didn't look upset, just frustrated. Annoyed.

Confused?

She was pointing at the handle of one of the doors, a heavy rusty one. It looked real, heavy, worn out.

Finally, it clicked.

"Yeah, sorry. I think so." My brain hurt, she seemed to be okay but my brain hurt and that awful, awful feeling. "Maybe they got out?"

The feeling telling me that I should stop, and keep going. To breathe but run because time was running out. But time to do what?

I put my hand on the handle, and this time it didn't disappear; it didn't melt.

It felt warm.

It fit perfectly on my hand.

Like it was meant to be.

She let go a sigh of relief, probably because she couldn't see my expression.

"Maybe this is it! It makes sense, right? I mean, it's the only door that looks actually used so I'd assume that the others..."

I couldn't keep listening to the sound of her voice.

I couldn't because it hit me.

The same fucking feeling from the bus.

Fuck. Fuck. Fuck. Fuck. Fuck.

No!

The doorknob started twisting underneath my hand and I couldn't let go. It was stuck to my skin. And twisted. And twisted.

Until we heard a click.

Fuck.

Fuckfuckfuckfuckfuckfuck

Fuckno

No

NonoNoNonOnOnonononNo

She finally saw my face, and hers twisted into a panicked reflection of how I felt.

"No!" She finally screamed what my mouth wouldn't let me say, and grabbed onto my other hand. Hard. Trying to pull me away.

I tried to run, to scream.

"Jasper, don't you DARE LEAVE ME ALONE AGAIN!"

I wouldn't.

I would never.

I tried to speak, to at least explain to her it wasn't my fault. That I was trapped, stuck to that goddamned fucking door.

Then it opened, and I felt weightless.

She screamed.

I couldn't.

Little by little, I started losing control over my body until my vision gave in and started to blur, but I couldn't know if it was because of the force pulling me inside or the tears drowning me.

Her hand slipped.

I tried to run one last time, but reality was shrouded in fog that turned me to stone.

I was only able to see Chiara's body lying on the ground for a split second before I opened my eyes.

In my bed, inside my bedroom.

Wishing her hand was still holding mine.

10
Crisis and Despair

No!!

               No. No. No. No.

No!
Not again.

             Oh, please not again, no.

I can't. I can't take it.
It can't happen again, please, no, no.
      NO!

But I knew it before I opened my eyes. The sharp pain on my side, the stiff neck. The cuts on my legs that felt like bleeding, even though every time I looked at them, they seemed to be mere scratches.

Those seats were definitely not made for sleeping.

I tried to cry, but dreams didn't work like that. Apparently, nightmares didn't either.

I wished with all my might to open my eyes and find the sterile, boring, white ceiling of the small efficiency apartment I was barely able to afford.

          Was that really what I wished?
        Even if it meant never having met him?

Him.

Jasper.

The boy with the leather jacket and the bitter smell. The one with the cautious smile and wonderful grey eyes.

The stranger I met in a dream that turned into a nightmare, before I got a chance to really get to know him.

The guy who hugged me, who told me we were in this together.

The one who abandoned me for the second time.

Abandoned. Again.

By choice, or by force? He wasn't there anymore, and I was trapped in that prison on wheels that didn't even work because none of it was supposed to be real in the first place.

Why did I even trust him in the first place?

Just because he was pretty and had a pretty notebook and looked nice when the light touched his skin, and looked so mysterious and cool, writing down all his interesting thoughts while everyone on the bus was just being miserable all around?

He probably didn't even care about me; he probably just pitied me because when he came back, I looked like I had been run over by a tornado or something. That was the only reason why he put up with me, for sure. Because he couldn't find the way to his actual dreams.

But he hugged me.

He gave me his jacket.

He let me scream at him, and didn't get upset.

He told me we were in this together.

I got up and looked around, trying to recognize any of the faces of the fake people around me. My memory was hazy, the clock in the front was still broken, my side kept hurting because I slept in such a weird position.

How had I even gotten back here?

I remember his face, the pure panic behind his eyes when he turned around. He was swallowed by darkness; his hand had been so sweaty, so cold, so soft.

That couldn't have been on purpose.

At that point, that hope was the only thing I had.

But what else? What else? What else could I do?

One hundred.

Ninety-nine.

Ninety-eight.

That was it. Patience. I only needed patience to get out of there. Clearly, the **bus** hadn't liked that I had left, so it had brought me back. Maybe I just needed to wait.

Eighty-seven.

Eighty-six.

But I had never been good at waiting. I got in trouble way too many times for not being able to sit down in class like a "normal girl". Like a "well-behaved girl". Like a "proper girl".

Seventy-five.

And time wasn't even passing, so why would I try anyway? The broken clock, the sour taste in my mouth, it seemed like every single detail was there to torture me again and again.

Sixty-what?

Counting down backward was a stupid way to pass the time anyway.

It didn't help that I couldn't stop thinking about him. If he would still remember me when he woke up. If he meant it when he said we were in this together.

The tears finally caught up with my emotions. They blurred my eyes and itched my cheeks. I had put him in danger, whether I wanted to admit it to myself or not. Something was wrong about me. Something about this nightmare wanted to correct it, to get rid of the impurities of what probably would have been a wonderful dream for him.

I couldn't wait for him to come back. What if he did? What if he got hurt even worse the next time?

It wasn't his fault that I was broken, even if I didn't really understand it either.

It wasn't his fault the bus tried to kill me.

It wasn't his fault that the mechanical creatures in the basement tried to rip me apart.

Had he even seen their eyes? The way they glowed?

I had to go. Escape this mess before he got entangled with my misfortune again. I knew deep down he had meant every word; I had *felt* it coming out of his skin.

I needed to get away from him as soon as I possibly could.

That was what got me moving. Not the impending doom, the nightmare, the claustrophobia, and knowledge I was trapped, chased. It was him, wanting him to be okay. Safe.

He had given me his jacket.

This was my jacket for him.

I started grabbing any possible heavy item I could find. I knew already the fake zombies wouldn't mind if I stole from them, so at least that part was easy.

The biggest backpack I saw, from one of the men in the back. Smaller purses inside. Books, notebooks that would never have the magnetic pull Jasper's had, shoes, water bottles. Everything, anything.

Things that wouldn't fit would be tight, but not impossible.

I filled it, and filled it, and filled it. Heavier by the second, I could barely drag it from the floor.

I was finally trying to close the second zipper and buckle it when I heard it. The screech of rusty metal that desperately needed lubrication. I turned around, almost involuntarily.

The mirror in the front was pointed directly at me, reflecting the bus driver's distorted face at an odd angle. Staring.

I managed to lift the backpack with both hands and swing it with my body, hitting it against the glass on the back door. And then again. And again. And again. It bounced and hit me. I pushed it with a scream and kept it going. Swinging it. Hitting it. My muscles ached and my legs burned, but I had to keep going. I needed to get out.

A crack on the glass.

I pushed through the purple starting to clog my fingers, the hot air burning my lungs. I had to leave before he came back. I couldn't bear to put him in danger again. Who was I trying to fool?

Crack.

He already meant so much more to me than he should have, without even knowing him; of course, he was going to continue to mean that much more now that I had met him. We had hardly spoken. We had met in the worst possible circumstances. Even if it was all half of a lie because, in theory, we hadn't even seen each other while awake.

Crack. Crack.

Nothing mattered, nothing except him. And I had to get out of there because if Jasper came back, and I was there, and something happened to him because of me, I would never forgive myself.

He had already said it once. The bus had been his way to ground himself. He'd be okay again without me.

A bigger crack.

The sound of a gruff and distorted voice echoed through the front of the bus. Loud, like a police siren coming through a megaphone. It came from all around me, from every single passenger, maybe from the seats as well.

The cracks wouldn't give in, and the **bus** seemed to be going faster now.

"Waatcha doooing doooown theeere?" The voice asked, elongating the sounds like it wasn't sure they were correct. It hit me like millions of bees, stinging into every single exposed pore.

My mouth filled with screams reduced to shreds by fragments of fog that began to seep through the cracks in the windows. The cracks on the door.

I looked back while still swinging, still hitting.

No, no. It couldn't be.

It hadn't.

Last time it hadn't moved.

The passengers stayed put this time, but the driver had left his post and was slowly moving towards me. Shuffling his feet, swinging his arms as he had just learned how to use his limbs. His torso swiveled left and right, his head flopped all over the place, like his neck was not strong enough to hold it.

More cracks. More. More.

All the pain I felt in that moment just fueled me. All the rage of being trapped there. The fear of what would happen if that excuse of a person got to me.

His nails clawed against my arm the second before the glass gave in. Propelled out of the door, tumbling over myself like a deflated balloon. The backpack went flying far. The scrapes on my legs and arms were actually bleeding this time. The tears burned my eyes and my mouth and, what?

And then ran.

My heart beat so fast I thought it was going to stop, that I was going to ironically die of an adrenaline overdose. My feet hit the ground harder and harder, faster and faster. It was like the ground was a never-ending treadmill that I couldn't get off of.

I knew that if I stopped running, I would fall forward. So, I kept going.

The night sky was deep purple this time, stars twinkled in green radioactive hues wherever I looked. Instead of reaching an arid, desolated place like last time, I was in the middle of... something.

A city?

Tall, twisting constructions surrounded me; they looked like glitches in a screen. I ran until my lungs ached, and then I ran some more. Ran past a gate that seemed to be stuck in itself, constantly going up and down. Ran past cars stopped in the middle of the road, with their lights on and no one at the wheel. Ran past stores that said they were open but had no doors.

And when I couldn't run anymore, I let myself finally fall to the ground.
If I died, I wanted those neon stars to be the last thing I saw.
No one came for me.
Everything was quiet, still.
I knew better than to feel good because of that.

Eventually, I started walking again. What else was I supposed to do? I learned there was a clock on every single wall, all of them broken at the same point. Even in the ones that appeared empty, at least one of them was slipping through the cracks, smaller than one of my nails.

None of them ticked.
Stuck.

*Like me, on that **bus**.*

The few doors I could find were fully open, almost inviting. Too suspicious.

I finally caved in and went inside one of the buildings through a ground-floor window instead.

As if that made it any better.

An insane amount of boxes, scattered all around. Piled up like someone was moving in. Or moving out. I had seen them before through the glass that looked like mist. Everything seemed to be in between states. Like the entire world was caught up in the middle of existing, and now it was pretending everything was fine.

There were things scattered out of the boxes. I approached one and felt the same magnetic sensation as with every object that had belonged to someone. More broken clocks, a watch, a stuffed animal, a white lighter, a statuette of a bird with red cheeks, a half-drunk bottle of water, headphones.

Amidst all that silence, the murmur of something different.
Music.

I picked up the headphones, connected to an old-fashioned fuchsia MP3 player. Exactly like the one I had when I was little.

How was I capable of remembering a stupid detail like that, but not when the last time I went to work was?

I felt watched, but I couldn't run anymore. My feet were on fire, my legs felt like crumbling down, my throat was ripping itself apart.

I closed my eyes and brought the headphones close to my head; the music seemed to finally slow my heartbeat.

I put them on and a wave of electricity filled me from head to toe. Nothing major, not a shock. Just a buzz, like little ants tickling my skin.

Without realizing it at first, I was walking again. Calm. My feet to the beat of the music. Out of the building, roaming the streets. I felt weightless, ethereal.

That music made everything more bearable, like things would be okay.
Like my feet weren't bleeding.
Like my side didn't hurt that much.
Like the clocks weren't broken.
Like my eyes weren't sunken in in the reflection of every window.
Like things would finally be okay.

11
Jinxed by Fate

"I didn't know you bit your nails." Leo's voice almost made me jump out of the chair.

It was the first minute of calm in what had proven to be a nightmare day. I had enough of nightmares already.

"Me neither," I responded, trying to brush it off and forcing my hand to separate from my mouth. Trying to smile. He walked up to me.

The aroma of his cologne penetrated my nostrils; his was the only one that never bothered me.

Because he was special.

Was.

"Damn, was it that bad?" He asked, putting a hand on the back of my chair. I had to desperately look inside the corners of my brain to try to figure out what he meant.

Oh, right.

Work.

"I hate printers. Why do they need paper in accounting anyway? Everything they do is online."

A blanket statement was good. Better than telling him I couldn't remember how to set them up in the first place because the only thing I could think about was if she hated me.

Of course she did. I left her alone.

But it wasn't my fault.

"Just a couple of hours, dude. We got this!" He said with a smile and to my surprise didn't really try to leave. He hesitated for a second and then started again. "So... I think I'm gonna go get a late lunch with Kevin and Noelle after work. Wanna come by?"

It wasn't my fault. But that didn't matter.

She was alone.

She...

Late lunch?

"Sure!" My mouth said the word faster than I could think. Leo smiled and went back to his desk. His cologne still permeated the air.

It wouldn't be the first time we went out to eat together, but it had always been a work thing, and he had never invited me himself.

But I couldn't, I had to go home and force myself to sleep.

I had to check in on Chiara.

I had to make sure she was okay.

I had to convince her not to hate me.

I had to—

Two hours passed, and we were eating at some Latin American fusion place.

"These are *maduros*, right?" Kevin asked, pointing at the plantains on his plate.

"We call them *tajadas*, but every country is different," I responded with a shrug.

It was easy to pretend to be part of a group, just let the conversation go, and only respond whenever someone made direct eye contact with me. Bonus points to me, because I always avoided eye contact with almost everyone. But today, I couldn't even focus on Leo's long eyelashes and big hands.

Why was I even there?

Why was I laughing and pretending I was fine when the universe inside my head was decomposing every second?

Why did I stay so long?

Why couldn't I just forget the whole fucking damned thing?

By the time I got home, it was already dark. I had spent the entire ride wishing desperately for a break. I couldn't fucking live like that! It was happening again, I could feel it in my bones.

Addiction.

Obsession.

"Dreams are not reality. Reality *is* reality," I repeated out loud the stupid mantra I had come up with when I was a teenager.

But it wasn't just a dream. There was her, an actual living person inside of it, and she was in fucking danger. She was in danger, and I left her alone because I was an idiot and touched that fucking door, and she probably hated me or got attacked by something or was fucking dead, and like, what the fuck was supposed to happen when you died in your dreams? Because people said that you woke up but she couldn't wake up in the first place so it could mean actually dying. And what if she was dying right at that moment and I couldn't save her because I was too late? Because I had stayed playing pretend with a group of coworkers I barely knew, just because one of them is hot and has talked to me a bunch of times and treated me decently?

I could rarely fall asleep the second I put my head on the pillow, but that night was the worst one of them all.

Thoughts raced through my head so much that no matter how many boxes I tried to put them in, how many times I counted my breath, how many attempts at meditation I did, nothing worked.

It was probably 2am when I finally got back on the bus. I jolted up immediately and looked around desperately.

"Chiara? Chiara!"

My heart dropped when I saw no signs of the redhead.

A gentle breeze coming from one of the open windows caressed my cheek; I took a deep breath and let myself fall to the seat next to me.

For the first time in a while, I felt calm.

I had done it. I was back on the bus again, with no one to bother me, to attack me, to talk to me.

I could listen to my own heartbeat, to my own thoughts. I could breathe.

Even my notebook was there, waiting for me. Everything back to normal. Just how I had wished for it.

That had to mean she was okay, right?

I caressed one of the pages with the graphite on my pencil.

Maybe I can write for a moment.
Just to calm my brain.
If she's not back at the bus, she's probably okay.
Maybe she finally woke up.

The words flew out of my hands so quickly I could barely keep up. For the first time I wrote about my dreams with the same detail and vehemence as I did about my day, trying to dissect piece by piece. Trying to understand how I felt, what went wrong, what went right.

What to do next.

Every time my thoughts went back to her I saw her distorted reflection again.

The blood.

The screams inside my brain.

After the third time, I woke up.

What?

The apartment was quiet, dark. Ominous.

I walked to the bathroom to pee and almost fell asleep while sitting on the toilet.

Washed my hands, got some water. Went to bed.

Closed my eyes.

The bus came quickly this time.

The notebook.

The thoughts.

Her.

I woke up again.

I looked at my phone screen, it had been an hour. I closed my eyes and tried again, made sure to not even move a muscle, to regulate my breathing, to do all the things you were supposed to do.

The bus.

The notebook.

Her.

The dark ceiling of my bedroom.

One more time.

And another.

And another.

And another.

And another.

And another.

Until I eventually spent the entire night sleeping in one-hour intervals.

What the actual fuck was going on?

The pounding headache I felt the morning after was insufferable. It came with the knowledge that something was *still* wrong. Why, if it wasn't, would I be booted out of my dreams like that every time she came to mind?

That ache in my chest kept telling me I had made a horrible mistake by choosing to stay, to write down my day and pretend nothing was wrong. It was accusing me of abandoning her, this time intentionally. The bus being so quiet, the open window I never noticed. The missing jacket reminding me she was real after all.

Maybe that's why I did it.

Not maybe, that IS why I did it.

I ran to the pharmacy after work and walked around the aisles like I didn't know exactly where the sleep aid was. My brain kept trying to convince me to let it go, to leave, to take a bath or something, maybe some tea. Something, the pull, that awful feeling that something was wrong, kept me going.

I felt sick when I grabbed it, like I was somehow losing all the progress I had made in years. My skin started itching, I wanted to cry. Thankfully no one was around me, because why on earth would the random dude in aisle six have an anxiety attack just because he was holding a fucking purple bottle?!

I asked for a paper bag, like I was ashamed.

Because I was.

Desperate.

At least that time I wasn't addicted to dreams. At least I still knew the difference between them and real life. I just needed extra help, something to calm me down, to bypass whatever it was that woke me up the night before.

To find her.

I ate a microwave dinner and took a deep breath, trying to quiet my brain and silence the stupid song I had stuck in my head. My hands were shaking when I measured the sleep-aid liquid on the cap - not one drop more, not one less.

I drank it in a gulp and sat in bed, with my notebook in my hand. A real one, the counterpart of the one I always brought to my dreams. I loved the sound of the pages turning, the way they rustled slightly, as if whispering secrets. In another situation, it would have probably calmed me down.

I wrote the same sentence over and over, trying to capture her essence. I focused on her face, trying to conjure up every detail, the exact shade of green of her eyes, the perfect amount of freckles.

Did she have moles?

How white were her teeth?

"I will find Chiara in my dreams tonight."

She was driving me insane, the whole situation was. Trying to get away was futile, idiotic. Every second that passed without knowing if she was okay, felt like nails crawling under my skin.

"I will find Chiara in my dreams tonight."

I wrote until my knuckles were on fire. Until the whole side of my left hand was dark grey from graphite. Until the entire English language stopped making sense and I started writing in Spanish.

"*Voy a encontrar a Chiara en mis sueños esta noche.*"

La músi—

The music, that fucking song, still hammered my senses. I had no clue where I had heard it first, it was almost like it appeared out of nowhere.

Like the screams.

The blood.

The next time I opened my eyes, I was on the bus.

Calm, quiet, like the day before. Still without my jacket, still with the notebook in my hand.

Still no Chiara.

The bus was riding slowly through a maze of buildings, gently, calmly. The breeze caressed me again and I had to physically shake the deja-vu from taking over me, before I made the same mistakes I had the last time. I turned to look behind me and the wave of realization of how fucking blind I was hit me so strongly I almost fell.

A mess of glass on the floor. A missing window.

She hadn't woken up.

It had to be her.

The pull came back twice as strong, as if to prove my point.

Chiara was somewhere out there, but how the fuck was I going to find her?

"*I will find Chiara in my dreams tonight.*"

I closed my eyes and bit my tongue, even though that hadn't worked before. My thoughts went to her, free to conjure her image, to mimic her voice. I tried to expand my reach through all possible corners of this dream that truly wasn't mine anymore. Tried to find her, use the fucking abilities I had perfected when I was addicted to a life that wasn't real.

The screams inside my brain, again.

The blood.

Her face, distorted into something awful.

And that fucking stupid song.

Even in such a serious situation, my brain still sabotaged me.

Of course it did.

I opened my eyes, there was fog outside the windows but I could still see the lights from the buildings around us. Shining from cracks on the walls.

I tried to feel something and for a second, there it was. The pull, the thing that would always tell me when my stop would come. The one thing Chiara never felt and—

That FUCKING SONG AGAIN?!

I drove my hands to my head and...

The song was getting louder.

The pull was getting stronger.

It tugged at me so hard it drove me to the back of the **bus.**

The song.

The pull.

The piece of shit bus that wasn't stopping for the first time in my life.

"Hey!" I screamed to the front without thinking too much about it. "Stop. That's my stop!"

My stomach dropped, I looked around, no one moved. No zombies trying to attack me like how they attacked Chiara. No screams. Nothing out of the ordinary.

"YO. STOP. THIS. NOW!" I screamed louder and banged at the door. The song started lowering its volume, the pull got weaker.

"STOP THIS MOTHERFUCKING BUS RIGHT NOW!" My voice almost burned my throat and I pulled at the cord so violently I actually ripped a bit off.

The driver's eyes met me through the rearview mirror, but he didn't move.

"Don't do it, kid." He said, with a voice that sounded too familiar for my taste. "It's not your time yet."

He didn't get up, no one else moved. The bus came to an abrupt halt in the middle of the street, no stop in sight. I looked at the piece of the cord I had ripped.

Maybe, I *could* control parts of this dream somehow.

Maybe, I had it all wrong. What if Chiara wasn't just the target before?

What if she was the only one out of both of us who could get hurt?

"Fuck you" I whispered as I pushed the door and forced it to open.

Then I ran all the way back.

I let the song guide me, let it deafen me while I tried to dodge the buildings. The beat grew accompanied by a soft tic-toc of clocks encrusted in the grey walls. All of them running at the same pace, as if time was even real in a place like this, all of them pointing at different numbers.

My feet pounded against the pavement with a sour taste in my mouth.

The green of the stars above me reminded me of her eyes and I just couldn't— I needed to find her. She had to be close. I couldn't lose her again.

The music grew louder and louder until I couldn't hear the tic-toc anymore, until the only thing that existed were the stars and the enormous grey walls at my sides.

"I will find Chiara in my dreams tonight."

I could have sworn I felt her somehow, somewhere in the middle of that attempt of a city. But the louder the music grew, the fainter the feeling was.

I kept thinking about her face.

The blood.

Something felt so horribly wrong and no matter how much I scanned the streets for her, how much I screamed, I couldn't. I just couldn't.

But I had to.

"I will find Chiara in my dreams tonight."

An orange dot on the horizon gave me the strength I didn't really have anymore. I ran even faster, my legs burning so much they would probably fall off at any second.

"Chiara!" I screamed at the top of my lungs. The orange dot didn't move.

"Chiara!"

She was there, sitting in the middle of a thin alleyway, still.

No, not still.

I got closer, the orange dot was bouncing almost imperceptibly.

The fucking song was about to rip my brain out of my skull, it reverberated through my bones.

"CHIARA!"

She was... bobbing her head?

I got close enough to see her. Her eyes had a haunted look, glazed over, lost somewhere far away from us. Her head was moving up and down at the rhythm of the clocks.

The rhythm of the song that had been tormenting me the whole day.

She had a horrifying smile on her face.

Something bright and pink shined in her hand. I cut the distance between us and almost threw myself at her, yanking it from her. The headphones she had been wearing fell out and the music stopped abruptly.

Her eyes focused again.

She came to.

"It's okay" She whispered through her teeth, still with that same unreal smile. Her eyes and cheeks were sunken, her skin had started to lose color. She looked almost... No. I couldn't think about that. "Things are going to be okay now."

12
Chaos Interconnected

It was such a nice song.
It made my body feel weightless.

Slow disintegrating.

Nothing around me mattered. The clocks, the walls. All a blur. I was back again in my room, with my things. Back when I first moved on my own.

"We'll hang out all the time!" Annie had texted me that day. "One hour is not that far, trust me. It's nothing!"

But best friends sometimes were the best because you saw them almost every day. Maybe all best friends were tied to a time and place.

The warmth of independence cocooned me. I missed my puppy, sure, but I had the rest of my life ahead! A place on my own, my first *big girl job*.

The music was the warmth. It made my skin feel soft and nice. It helped with the pain on my side.

I was now waiting at my stop for the first time. With full glam and a smile, checking myself constantly on my phone screen as if it were a mirror.

Another memory.

The bus arrived and I double-checked the number.

Twelve.

The driver had been nice that day. They weren't always nice. Sometimes they—

It was over.

Something had ripped it away from me.

The music was gone.

The cold came back.

The pain.

The world.

The boy.

Jasper.

He looked sad, worried. Didn't he know things were going to be okay?

"It's okay," I whispered, and my voice sounded dry, unnatural. "Things are going to be okay now."

I was so tired all of a sudden. All that thinking, all those memories.

Too much energy.

Sleeping sounded nice. So nice.

"Chiara!" His scream shook me awake; his hands helped.

"I was in the past," I said, and my head started throbbing. "The bus. I was taking the bus."

"I woke up again. And again. It's been two days, Chiara." He held me in his arms, and I buried my face in his chest. "I'm so fucking sorry. I swear I didn't know. I should have never touched that fucking door. I'm so sorry. I didn't know. I didn't..."

We both dissolved in a mess of sobbing and half-muttered words in our attempt to understand whatever was happening around us, to us.

It was a puzzle, a threat, and a joke all at the same time.

Stupid, absurd, chaotic.

Like us.

Putting the pieces together at least kept my mind distracted from that warmth.

The feeling of just wanting to let go.

Let go of what, exactly?

"Are you sure it's the same song?" he asked, and I nodded.

"Look into my eyes, and tell me what you feel," I hummed. *"For moments like these, falling drops are enough."*

"If they were the price," he completed the line. *"I'd let myself dry just to feel you."*

I nodded.

We were walking through the skeleton of that thing that should have been a city. My eyes were fixed in front of us, Jasper's arm still around my shoulder; his eyes on me.

He looked exhausted, still worried.

Something was wrong.

Every time I tried to look at a window, a door, a puddle on the floor, every time my eyes floated to something even remotely reflective, he would distract me.

I wasn't stupid, but pretended I was.

My reflection was the last thing I wanted to look at.

"I can't believe every time I try to do anything in this nightmare, I get actual monsters, and you just get a mild frown of disapproval," I said instead. Jasper chuckled, but the laugh was dry.

"I wish it would attack me too," he started. I stopped completely and jerked him backwards, his arm still refusing to leave me.

"No, you don't. Don't try to be a martyr. It sucks, but there's clearly something wrong with me. Would you rather something be wrong with both of us?!" It all came down at once, crushing me with its weight. "At least you were able to find me!"

My legs faltered, and he helped me stabilize.

My side started aching again.

My cheeks burned with tears.

He held me for what felt like a lifetime. Didn't say a word, just stood there with his eyes closed, holding all the broken pieces of myself together.

My eyes kept finding shadows moving in irregular motions; their silhouettes were hazy, glitching. Every time I saw a new one, I hugged Jasper tighter and tighter. The skin on his neck was soft, and I rested my cheek against it. The stubble on his chin tickled my forehead.

I pulled away for a second, just a few inches, and looked into his eyes.

We were close, so close it hurt.

His breath and mine mingled, intertwined like us.

He opened his eyes and smiled when he saw mine. His hands still held me, afraid I would fall if he didn't.

He looked exhausted; stress had drained the color from his cheeks.

Stress that I had caused.

But it wasn't my fault.

Neither of us dared to even move. This universe of lies that surrounded us seemed to hate us, and I feared that if we took one more step in the wrong direction, it would destroy us before we knew it.

Jasper smiled with quivering lips, one of his hands moved to my shoulder and caressed it. His fingers were trembling too. He was shaking all over because of me.

It wasn't my fault. But that didn't matter.

Each of my senses began to scream at me over and over again when I pulled away. He looked at me, confused for a couple of seconds, and then pulled away too.

So fast that I felt a twinge in my chest.

Better that way.

Too much damage had already been done.

We walked in silence, still not knowing where we were going, for what seemed like hours. I had to stop to catch my breath more times than I wanted to admit. My feet were on fire. Everything hurt, burned.

The cracks on the walls were still adorned with clocks that had stopped forever, the stars had become silver dots.

Like his eyes.

Jasper caught my gaze and, perhaps because the silence was as unbearable for him as it was for me, he came closer and began to talk to me again.

My heart hurt a little less thanks to his voice.

"I know, they're extremely annoying," he said, pointing at the clock I had been staring at.

We were at the edge of the city at that point; most of those awful, broken omens were left behind. At least the noticeable ones.

"It's just broken clocks," I responded with a shrug. "At least they're not—"

"Ticking," he completed my sentence, wide eyed. "They *are* ticking. At least for me, they are. Loud, so loud it's unbearable to listen to."

Not again.

Not another incomprehensible detail that might mean something or be pointless.

Not another piece of a puzzle we didn't even know if we were supposed to complete.

No.

No.

"No," my voice came out confused. "Not loud. Not for me." I shook my head, trying to find the right words. "I see them broken, stuck at the same time. Like the one on the bus."

"The clock on the bus was working for me, too. It didn't tick as loudly, but definitely worked," he said, walking towards the wall and extending a hand as if he was about to touch it. "What time does it say?"

"Six forty-two."

I took a couple of steps back, suddenly wanting to put as much distance between myself and the wall as possible.

That weird clock between the cracks.

Jasper brought a finger close to one of the hands and tried to move it, but he pulled his hand away with a sharp groan. I jumped back, and my legs bumped into something.

"Son of a bitch, it bit me," he whispered, looking at his finger.

I burst out laughing; I couldn't help it.

A clock! A clock hand had bitten his finger!

If I hadn't been so exhausted, if the danger that seemed increasingly imminent wasn't lurking in the shadows I could still see out of the corner of my eye, I would have thrown myself on the floor laughing.

My legs bumped into the same thing behind me. I turned around, holding my side, which was aching now because of the laughter.

"Oh no. Hell no. No. No. No!" I tried to run, but Jasper caught me in his arms again.

This time the pressure was different, no longer this comforting warmth that swore things would be okay. Now he was making sure I wasn't running away.

Why?

Was it his fault all along?

Did he know something I didn't?

I was an idiot for trusting him. He was probably working with the shadows. He was taking me somewhere, he—

"This stop looks different," he said, and turned me around.

I was overreacting; he was right.

It was a metal bench surrounded by three metal walls, with an arched mirror covering it like a roof. It reflected the city behind us, the silver stars, the deep blue of the night sky.

The stop would have been yellow in another life, but it was covered in so many scribbles it almost looked entirely black.

"Maybe it's not the same **bus**," he whispered, gently letting go of me. "Sorry. I really thought I was going to lose you again for a second."

"It might be," I forced myself to walk away from him. Slowly, making sure he understood I didn't want to leave. Even though the fear started creeping in. "But you should go."

"Chiara," he pleaded.

I heard him through the tears blurring my vision.

"You should wait for the **bus** and go, because you deserve to go to sleep and be in your dreams instead of whatever this nightmare is. And we both know it's my fault." My cries grew louder and louder. "You haven't shaved, and you look sick, and it's not worth it. You barely know me. This is all so stupid."

"Go where?" His words carried all the exhaustion I saw in his eyes. "I can't even focus on a single conversation while I'm awake because I can't stop thinking about you, Chiara." This time, he didn't walk to me, almost like he was afraid I would try to run if he dared.

"I got a taste of normalcy when I opened my eyes on the **bus** again. But you weren't there." He was fiddling with his nails, looking everywhere but where I was standing. "I don't... I don't want dreams without you in it."

My mouth dried up.

My heart sank.

I took a single step towards him, and all of a sudden, he looked terrified. Of me?

Of whatever I felt?

"Jasper, it's not fair to you."

"I don't care about fairness. I wrote your name over and over in my notebook, because something inside me couldn't bear not seeing you again."

I took another step, but he still didn't move.

He looked ashamed, vulnerable.

I wanted to hold him, to tell him how I felt. But I didn't even have the answer to that.

"I got so happy when I saw your face again," I whispered, not sure what I was even trying to say with that. "And I'm so happy to know you didn't abandon me, but I can't just drag you along into my mess. We both know it's me who has the problem."

"We're connected, we have to be," he interrupted me. A slight breeze that smelled of ocean air enveloped us. "I heard the song that came out of those headphones," he pointed at them, peeking out of my pocket. "I felt a pull that brought me to you time and time again. The same pull that's telling me now to sit and wait." He paused and extended a hand towards me. "Together."

He was special.

And I was selfish.

So I held his hand, and he pulled me towards him.

He put his hands around my neck and touched my forehead with his.

His lips were chapped.

His bitter smell, tangled with the breeze.

The soft breeze that all of a sudden became a strong wind that pulled us apart.

Like a metaphor for what the world did to us each time.

A breeze that now brought a third smell with it. A dangerous one.

"Something's burning," he said before I could.

I held his hand again, ready to run. The smell was getting stronger by the minute, but he stayed with his feet planted on the ground.

"No, we can't leave. We have to stay here and wait."

"Are you crazy?"

The sky slowly began to turn red.

His whole body shuddered and he let go of my hand so quickly that I could have sworn he had been electrocuted. He knelt on the ground and began to trace the scribbles that decorated the walls of the bus stop.

"Jasper. Jasper, it's the city," I said, and a wave of heat almost overwhelmed me.

"Wait a second. I swear there's something here," he replied, now kneeling on the bench, searching for something among the red hinges that held it together.

I could run, save myself. The worst that could happen to him would be to wake up, but everything indicated that I wouldn't have the same chance.

Something like a snowflake landed on my nose, and I immediately sneezed.

No, not a snowflake.

Ashes.

"I knew it!" he shouted, standing up and waving me over.

We were going to die, because if it wasn't me doing stupid things, it was him.

We were going to die like two idiots because Jasper thought it would be cool to study graffiti in the middle of a fire that was going to engulf us at any moment.

"Look!" he insisted, until he jogged over to me and pulled me by the arm.

My heart stopped in the middle of that bad joke.

But how could I run and leave him there?

After everything we'd been through together?

After it was clear we were connected?

"When I was little, I carried markers everywhere. I used to carve my initials into anything I could find. Trees, park benches, the walls of buildings, anything." He started pointing at the lines in the stop.

The smell was almost burning through my nostrils, the ashes started to melt against my skin.

"How is this going to save us from being burned down along this stop, Jasper?" I couldn't cry anymore; the fear had dried up my tears.

It was too late to run; my legs reminded me how tired they were and were ready to give up one more time.

Maybe it was time to give up, to let go.

I eyed the MP3 player and considered putting the headphones on again, just so the music could help me forget.

Deep down, I knew what that meant.

The memories.

The numbness.

"It's the pull again." He grabbed something from his back pocket, a marker. "It's telling me to do this."

He took off the cap and scribbled something on a small space that had no markings yet.

Something.

His initials?

JD.

Wait.

What?

No. It couldn't be.

I was imagining things.

"Jasper, what's your last name?" I asked, my entire body was trembling.

I should have realized it, I should have seen it coming.

"Dávila, why?" he responded without giving it too much importance, looking into the distance.

But it was important.

The most important thing.

It was everything.

The floor immediately started shaking and the smell of gasoline competed with the smoke.

JD.

"Let's go!" he said, pulling me towards the open doors of a bus.

I didn't even have time to fully comprehend what was happening.

"This doesn't make any sense," I whispered, letting myself be dragged.

Because he was right, and this whole thing was way bigger than just pure coincidences. My brain was still trying to process it all, so much so that the fire and the ashes seemed like a thing of the past.

Connected.

Tied together.

"We did it!" He was hugging me tight, kissing my cheeks again and again, but never my lips.

I shook my head to recognize we were inside a bus.

A different one from before.

This one was completely empty, except for the scribbles that covered the walls. Just like that bus stop.

Vibrant, colorful, they seemed to dance across the walls. Jasper had tears in his eyes and proudly pointed at all the little drawings.

"We did it!" He repeated, trying to make me react.

"Did what?"

He took his notebook out of a pocket that was too small to fit it in.

But dreams didn't have to make sense.

He opened the pages right in front of my face. The same scribbles that could have been text, the drawings of things that resembled hearts and faces.

He couldn't stop smiling.

"Chiara, we found the way back to my dreams!"

13
Jigsaw Pieces

My cheeks hurt like crazy, but I didn't care.

Finally, a break.

With her.

At last, something that showed us that perhaps all was not lost, that we might find actual answers.

Or at least we wouldn't be attacked again.

At least *she* wouldn't be attacked again.

She.

My head was still spinning, trying to make sense of a world that didn't need logic to survive.

I looked around at the walls and seats covered with my drawings. Every scribble, every word I had written in my notebooks was there. Some out in the open, others hidden, but there.

It was like looking inside my brain.

I tried to look away from the details I didn't want to remember, but for the most part, nostalgia overwhelmed me so strongly that I had to sit down.

"Are you okay?" she asked, sitting next to me.

No.

She was the one who needed to rest, the one who had to sit down and relax.

I should have been asking her that.

"I'm fine! How are you feeling?" My smile pulled too tight on opposite sides of my face. She furrowed her brow. "I'm fine, seriously. I know this has been a lot on you, though. How are you feeling right now?"

"I'm also fine, don't worry too much about me." Her voice trembled for a split second, her eyes were still sunken in.

"You look like shit, Chaira. Are you sure?" The words came out of my mouth so fast I almost tried to catch them with my hands.

That was so inappropriate.

I was a fucking idiot.

"Oh wow, thank you, I guess?" she responded, but laughed, and my stomach untwisted. She sighed. "It's nice to sit down, my legs are burning up." She bit her lip, then took a deep breath. "My side has been hurting a lot at random moments and I feel like something's wrong with my brain."

She pulled her feet up to the seat and hugged her knees. I didn't know what to do, so I put my arm around her shoulders.

Again.

Because what else was I supposed to do?

Her skin was soft and nice, but also cold. She was shivering and I didn't have my jacket anymore to give her comfort.

I just wanted to help her feel better.

I felt useless.

I was useless.

Still, she leaned her head on my shoulder and everything felt okay.

Her hair smelled of petrichor and frankincense. I closed my eyes and let it envelop me, transporting me to another reality for a moment. A dream within a dream, a perfect paradise covered by her freckles.

Her breathing slowed and deepened, and soft snores began to escape from her chest.

I couldn't help but smile.

At least she felt safe enough to rest.

We continued like this for seconds, minutes, hours. I took a deep breath too and started looking around me again. At the scramblings of myself trying to comprehend life one way or another. At the lists of tasks I had to finish the day after I wrote them. At the names of all the boys and girls I had liked throughout my life.

Including hers.

Over and over again.

Her name, camouflaged on seats, in corners, on the ceiling.

Another name was hidden among them, crossed out. The name of a person who no longer existed. I smiled.

I was myself now.

The bus slowed to a stop, in eternal contrast to the abruptness of the metal prison that had bound her before.

She opened her eyes and looked up. My shirt had left marks on her cheek. They danced along her freckles.

I smiled, she smiled back.

I could have kissed her.

I wish I had done it.

"Are you sure we're in the right place?" she asked me as we got off the bus, looking around in absolute shock.

"Yes," I replied, my voice breaking without me being able to help it.

Chiara took my hand and looked at me. I smiled and took a deep breath, using my free hand to wipe away my tears.

Around us was a city completely different from the one we had left behind. A valley, a mix of buildings and red-roofed houses. Streets with pavement made of intricate gradients that wound and disappeared among bushes and parks. Storefronts dressed up in tiles made of leaves.

Yellow trees with cayenne flowers as roots swayed in the wind. More birds than I could count. Large, enormous macaws. A mountain in the distance. Green, like Chiara's eyes.

A total cliché.

A mixture that might have seemed ridiculous to anyone who didn't understand it.

But it was perfect.

"Oh, Jasper? Jasper, are you okay?!" she asked me worriedly. I nodded, wiping away my tears again.

Fuck.

How I had missed this view.

"My mom and I moved to the US when I started high school," I explained, starting to walk through the giant boulevard in front of us. "You already know I lucid-dreamed a lot and… I missed my city."

She let go of my hand for a second, taking everything around us in. Then threw herself into my arms and hugged me so tightly I thought she'd ripped my spine in two.

"It must be awful to have to leave a place like this," she whispered in my ear. "I'm so sorry, I can't begin to imagine—"

I wrapped my arms around her waist and smiled.

"I'm glad I get to share it with you," I whispered in return.

Even if it was a distorted version of it. Even if my mind, with its rose-colored glasses, had made the colors more vibrant and covered the potholes on the streets. It was, in essence, Caracas.

The city that never saw me become an adult, but had never left my mind.

I let go when she started trembling.

"What happened?" I asked. She shook her head, and forced a smile. "Did you see something?" I looked around. "Is it fire? Did something follow us? Another monster?"

"It's shadows," her voice was barely above a murmur. "I've been seeing them, it's like the ones next to my bed when... You know."

"Sleep paralysis?" I asked. She nodded and started walking again. This time, I was the one who held her hand.

"It was right after you found me, after you took the headphones off." Her eyes wandered to everything around us, almost like trying to use the brightness of the environment as a shield. But she still shivered from time to time. Like something was lurking in the corners of her eyes. "Something... I think they did something more than just calling you with that song."

"What do you mean?"

"I can't remember things about my life well, but the headphones brought back memories. When I moved by myself, when I took my actual bus for the first time." Her voice was soft and calm. "I think they're part of the puzzle."

We stopped to sit on a bench. She took out the MP3 player and put the headphones on with a sigh.

The song immediately started playing inside my head again, her eyes glazed over once more.

And then...

What the actual fuck?!

The shadows on her face began to intensify but the light around us remained unchanged.

Her cheeks, which had gradually taken on color again during the bus ride, paled. Her eyes once again became sunken, with dark circles underneath.

It seemed.

No.
It couldn't be.
Not again.

I ripped off the headphones so hard they almost took one of her earrings with them. The song stopped immediately.

"Chiara!"

"It's peace. It's such a great feeling of peace, Jasper." Again with that smile that scared me more and more, the smile of someone who had stopped fighting. "This time I remembered a café, sometimes I would go there with my computer to work. Maybe if you put them on—"

"You look like a corpse!" Maybe I shouted too loudly. Nothing mattered.

I stood up and shook her, careful not to break her in two. I forced myself to ignore the retching I felt. I couldn't break, not when she clearly needed me.

"I what?" Her eyes were coming back to normal, but she still looked out of it.

"You looked dead! The second you put them on, you looked fucking dead!"

I was crying again.

Her chest started rising up and down, her breathing became more and more agitated, like an electric current had shocked her entire being.

Then she bent over, holding her side in pain.

The screams I had heard back at the house made of hallways came to haunt me once more. Drilling my skull.

And I remembered the blood.

Her distorted reflection.

I tried to hold her, but she jumped back.

"Something is happening to me!" she screeched and took a step back, then another. "My brain. My memories." Another step back, then pointed behind me. "That house!"

I turned around and shook my head. That wasn't supposed to be there.

The colors were different from the rest, more muted and devoid of life. It didn't have the beautiful red-tiled roofs or grated windows.

Boring.

Out of place with the rest of my beautiful, dreamlike Caracas.

Foreign.

"That's MY HOUSE!" she screamed and ran past me so fast I couldn't stop her.

Something twinkled on the pavement, still playing that fucking song.

I kicked it to the grass and ran past Chiara.

We didn't need that shit, not when it was sucking the life out of her like that.

"Why is my house in the middle of your dreams?" She looked agitated, confused, and immediately clung to my arm when she saw me.

I shook my head.

"This part doesn't feel like mine. Is this where you live right now?" I asked before having a chance to look around.

But then, I did.

The place wasn't empty, not entirely.

Shadows.

Silhouettes of something, of someone that was supposed to be there, were all around us.

They didn't seem to care that we had disrupted them, just moved from one place to the other, like the fake people in the main **bus**.

I couldn't move, couldn't breathe.

Chiara looked at me, then at them, then back at me.

"This is the house I grew up in," she responded in a whisper. "Now you see them too?"

I nodded and took a step towards the stairs. The shadows didn't move.

She followed though, still holding me tight.

Another step.

Then another.

Then another.

We passed by one of them, standing next to a rotary phone and speaking words that sounded muffled.

Still nothing.

"Well, it's the dream version of my house," she broke the silence after we realized we were safe from the shadows. "When I would dream about skinwalkers killing my parents, they were usually here."

I looked at the polaroids scattered through the stairs as we went to the second floor. The faces were distorted, but I'd recognize her orange hair anywhere.

Skinwalkers.

Nightmares.

Sleep paralysis.

No wonder she was so jumpy.

"That's traumatizing," I whispered. She chuckled and shrugged. "No, for real. How old were you when that happened?"

"I don't know, probably seven? I mostly have nightmares, so if it's not those, then it's other kinds of monsters or someone following me. The worst ones are when it's real people, you know? Like, one time I dreamed about these guys that were trying to harass this little girl and I ended up just bashing their heads in. It was so gross, I literally would feel their skulls caving in and..." She stopped when we reached the top floor and turned to see me. "Too much?"

I wanted to throw up.

"It's fine. I'm fine, just. Holy shit." I couldn't get any of those out of my head.

How were you supposed to live your life when every time you close your eyes, you saw shit like that?

Another shadow came out of one of the bedrooms, and I jumped; she didn't.

It was like her brain adapted to their awful presence.

Like she was used to them now.

"JD?" she called from the door of another room. I jerked my head towards her.

"You've never called me that" I responded, walking towards her.

"We've known each other for like, three days. It's not like there has been a lot of time for petnames." She was smiling again. "Wait, but is it okay? Because if it's not okay I'll stop. I just thought since... I mean, those are your initials, right? I figured it was okay but also it's relevant. I mean, your name. I think it's a piece. But I can stop and call you Jasper again if you want to. Or anything else you'd like."

The way her brain could compartmentalize all the insane bullshit around us and just keep going was terrifying.

And admirable.

I laughed and we both entered the room.

"JD is fine. What do you mean it's a piece?"

The walls were hot pink, as were the bed cover, cabinet doors, and all the decorations. Pale wooden furniture fitting together like it was also a puzzle.

Like our lives in that moment.

I looked at her in her edgy, all-black outfit and fishnets, then looked around again.

And smiled.

"Yep, it checks out," I couldn't help but say. She bumped my arm with her fist.

"What do you mean it checks out?!" She pretended to be offended, but her smile grew bigger.

"You definitely look like a pink girlie."

"Well, pink is a pretty color, but that's not what I wanted to show you!"

She sat on the bed and hugged one of the plushies while closing her eyes. Her smile faded slightly and her hand went to her side again for a second. She tried to play it cool, I pretended I didn't notice.

But my insides were burning.

I needed to help her.

I needed her to be okay.

"It's like my memory is being deleted backwards," she said after a few minutes. I sat next to her. "At least when I don't have the headphones on. I remember things that happened a while ago, but not recent ones."

"What did you want to show me?" I asked. She sighed.

"Don't think I'm weird, please."

"You're kind of weird already." My voice sounded harsh, fuck. "But I like you! I mean, I like it. I think you're cool, weird, and all."

She snorted and pushed the plushie against me.

"I think you're cool too. Weird and all."

Chiara kissed my cheek and kneeled on top of the mattress, opening one of the pink cabinets above the bed.

A pile of papers fell on top of her and she grabbed one of them.

"JD" she called me again. I tilted my head, waiting. "No, literally. JD."

She gave me the paper.

My breath skipped.

Over and over and over.

My initials filled the page.

I took one of the fallen papers, the same thing.

And another.

And another.

"Is this... recent?" I was afraid of the answer. She shook her head.

I stood up.

What the fuck was going on?

What did she know?

What was she not telling me?!

"Calm down!" She looked terrified all of a sudden. I couldn't really tell what my face was doing at the moment.

"Why do you have a million papers with my initials in your childhood bedroom?" I was trying to force myself to be calm, but holy shit, it was hard.

"When I was little..."

"Answer me!"

"I'm trying to! Listen. When I was little, I felt so lonely, and I read a lot. So many books about soulmates, about people that were destined to be together." Her voice was quivering again, and her eyes darted all around the room. "I wanted to have someone like that! You know? To know who my person was."

"What the fuck does this have to do with me?"

"I prayed, looked into divination, into angels, anything that would give me a clue, anything!" Her breathing became more and more agitated. She extended her hand to reach me, but I couldn't move. I couldn't think. "Eventually, I saw these two letters everywhere. I dreamed about them. They had to mean something, I just didn't know what."

Something was wrong; her eyes still darted all around. She was jumpy again.

And I felt it too. A looming sensation that we were getting close to something we weren't supposed to.

"Jessica Damon. Johannes Dordelly. Jocelyn Dunn." She closed the distance between us and this time took my hand without hesitation. "All my crushes, all my exes. JD. Don't you get it? Without meeting you, I've been looking for you my whole life."

Tears bathed her precious green eyes. Bloodshot, desperate.

We were connected, I felt it.

She felt it too.

This intense, insane string that pulled us together in ways that shouldn't be possible.

I cupped her face in my hands, counted each one of her freckles.

She was crazy.

I was crazy too.

Maybe we were meant for each other after all.

I closed my eyes and moved closer.

One second too late.

My lips only found a scream.

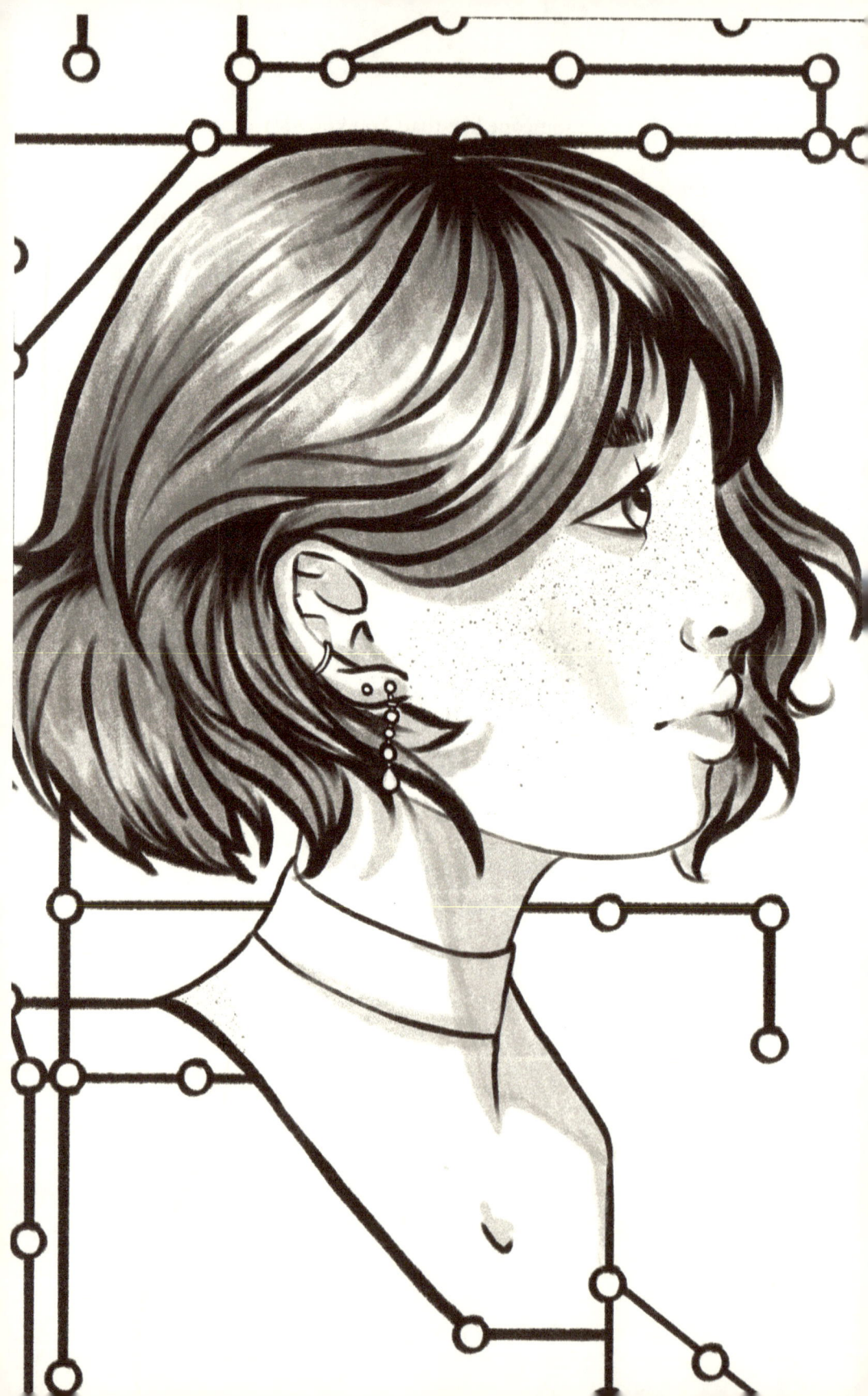

14
Coincidence or Fate?

He was freaking out, of course he was.

But he needed to see it, to understand that this was bigger than we thought!

I was an idiot for not thinking about it the second I heard his name, for not connecting the dots.

JD.

It was there all along!

All the times I had spiraled into trying to find someone's last name to see if it might be 'the one'. All the books and blog posts and videos about a million different ways to see into the future. All the dreams. All the times those two letters appeared in my life again and again.

It had all led to this moment.

To him.

To us.

He wasn't just a stupid passing crush I had. He wouldn't dissolve the second I gave him too much attention. He wouldn't disappear when I got bored because the chase was what kept me alive.

This was it.

"Without meeting you, I've been looking for you my whole life," I whispered.

My throat was on fire and my eyes hurt from crying too much, from feeling too strongly. I looked into his eyes and didn't see repulsion; that was something at least.

He didn't run away or scream at me.

His hands met my face and my entire being collapsed against his touch.

I tried to focus on his gaze, to pretend I didn't feel the cold filling the room, that I didn't see how dark everything got all of a sudden.

Maybe if we kept ignoring the shadows, they wouldn't do anything this time.

Maybe if we kissed, the curse would be broken.

Maybe, just for this time, life could actually be like in a movie.

He closed his eyes and I left mine open. I needed to see, to make sure they wouldn't get in between us.

Something on my side, a different type of cold, like algae at a beach.

Then on my back.

On my neck.

He moved closer, the shadows ripped me away from his hands.

The scream came almost immediately. An unstoppable, piercing sound that shattered the windows of the bedroom I spent most of my life as a child. The paper pages with Jasper's initials flew around us, covering his face.

Once again, the universe was trying to keep us apart.

Why?

Why?

Why?

Why? Why? Why?

Why? Why?

He jumped forward and used his notebook to hit the one that was trying to get into my nostrils. It smelled wet, rotten, dead. Suffocating. Disgusting.

It was easy to think that they couldn't really hurt him unprovoked, but what if they could when he was touching me? Helping me?

"You look like a corpse," he had said.

Was that what was really happening?

Was I dead already?

What was the point of keeping the fight then?

He grabbed a lamp and kept hitting them; they dissolved into a puddle of goo that burned the floorboards beneath us.

"Grab my hand!" Jasper's voice was barely audible above my screams, but I did what he said.

Even if it felt futile.

Useless.

Adrenaline kicked in the second I was freed from their grasp. We ran downstairs and kicked the door open in that weightless way that only makes sense in dreams.

Outside was almost worse.

That beautiful city that told me so much about Jasper without even needing to speak was slowly melting into the ground. There were holes in the asphalt, and the red tiles of the roofs crashed against the floor. The colors were slowly fading away, engulfed by shadows.

His entire universe was collapsing.

Because of me.

Me.

I was ruining his life, inside and out.

I tried to stop but he pulled me to keep running.

It was pointless.

But he kept going.

"I know you're tired. Just hold on a little longer!" he said with watery eyes, probably from seeing his sanctuary collapse around us.

Because of me.

Me.

"There are too many, we can't—" He didn't let me finish. At least one of us wasn't giving up.

"The subway!" he yelled instead and led me to a big yellow construction with an enormous red M on one side.

I was about to scream that there wasn't a door when the tubes that formed the station separated and opened a space big enough for us to go through. And immediately closed behind us.

The stillness was daunting.

I looked around every corner but the shadows looked still, lifeless. Maybe we were safe for a moment.

We still ran down the escalators and didn't stop until we were underground.

It was insane.

The ceiling was enormous, the place looked like it spanned several blocks. The floor had a strip of diagonal lines of colors that mixed and matched into others; they seemed like they had life on their own.

A rainbow made with green, red, black and blue.

"Oh my God, Jasper, is this how all subway stations look over there?!" I asked without being able to contain my shock.

He laughed.

In the middle of this madness, he laughed so loudly it reverberated against the walls.

"This is the airport!" he responded, like it was the best joke he had ever heard. "Holy shit, dreams truly don't make any fucking sense."

"I don't feel the shadows anymore," I said after we started walking at a somewhat normal pace.

His demeanor relaxed significantly and he let himself smile.

That beautiful, calm smile that made me believe that things were going to be okay.

I looked around me, taking everything in.

The gorgeous rainbow floors.

The empty lines to buy tickets from no one in particular.

The departure screens spewing nonsense.

The digital clocks everywhere pointing at the same time, like all the other ones I had seen.

The transit map on that wall that looked super familiar.

Familiar.

Because I recognized it.

It couldn't be.

"Hey JD, what's this?" I pointed at it, he came closer to take a look.

"I guess that's my brain's way to remember which bus routes to take," he shrugged, visibly calmer after not having to struggle against monsters to save me for at least half an hour. "This is where I live now. It's Upstate NY.

Not as fancy as the city, but it's fine for me."

"Riverholt," I said loudly, and he coughed.

"How do you...?"

"I live somewhere around here." My trembling finger pointed at a corner of the map. The silence engulfed us both. We couldn't dare say a word. "There's a new bus route that goes straight here, but it opened only a few days ago. That's what I saw the last time I put the headphones on."

"Holy fucking shit. This is it!" He started jumping up and down, then immediately stopped. Like he had done something shameful.

But it was adorable.

He was so adorable.

He deserved better than running around, escaping from monsters because of me.

Me.

Me.

"We're so close to each other. I can wake up and look for you! Chiara, I can find you!" He was trying so hard to contain his emotions. It gave me hope; maybe he was right. "But you have to tell me more details and we have to find a way to unscramble your brain, because this," he pointed at the route I mentioned, "hasn't opened yet."

"I'm absolutely sure, Jasper. I literally saw that memory right before you told me I looked dead." I traced the lines exactly where the bus would pass. It was the clearest thought in my mind. "This is really weird. How didn't we even think about the possibility of living in the same place?" My chest started hurting, I held on to the wall to not fall.

He sat on the floor and smiled. I did the same. It was cold, but not like the unnatural feeling of the shadows eating me alive.

It felt nice, refreshing.

"We're connected," he said and held my hand. "We just need to find out how much."

"Tell me about yourself." I hugged my knees and rested my cheek on one of them.

It was stupid to try to get to know him when it was becoming clear by the minute that my life was in danger.

But maybe that's why it was so important to know who he was, to cherish those details before it was too late.

He smiled and put a strand of hair behind my ears.

"I went to Catholic school, but I'm not really religious. I hated the uniforms though, and the girls were mean as shit," he let out a dry laugh. "When we moved I didn't have a lot of friends so I spent most of my time online. I joined these roleplay forums where you would start a story and other people would chime in."

My laughter cut him off.

"One of my friends begged me to join one. But I always forgot to answer threads." This was nice, almost normal. "Krolica, I think. I never knew someone else who used to do those things."

He paled.

"That's it. That's where I spent most of my life for like… Two years, I think." His eyes moved rapidly, like he was doing mental math. Something had clicked inside his brain and I was trying to process it as quickly as possible, but still didn't get it.

What was it?

What was it?

What was it?

"Uhm… Let me think. When I was sixteen, I joined this writing contest. It was for a video game that never got produced. I got second place because a last-minute entry won the first prize." It looked like he was physically trying to pull the memories out of his brain. "Clear Wounds and Open Skies."

Pain.

So much pain.

My head felt like it was splitting in two.

Could it be?

"Was it a dating sim?" I asked and started sweating. Jasper nodded and gulped. "I… I won that. I got some airpods in the mail because of it."

"This is fucking insane."

It was absurd, how we seemed to be made for each other and yet never met before.

How the nooks and crannies of his life fit so perfectly in mine.

The silence helped everything sink in, like a calm ocean before tides started rising.

Tides that would engulf us if we kept going.

Buy why?

Why?

Why? Why? Why? Why? Why? Why? Why? Why? Why? Why? Why? Why? Why? Why? Why? Why? Why? Why? Why? Why? Why? Why? Why? Why? Why? Why? Why? Why? Why? Why?

Why? Why? Why? Why? Why? Why? Why? Why? Why? Why? Why? Why? Why? Why? Why? Why? Why? Why? Why? Why? Why? Why? Why? Why? Why? Why? Why? Why? Why? Why? Why? Why? Why? Why? Why? Why? Why? Why? Why? Why? Why? Why? Why? Why? Why? Why? Why? Why? Why? Why? Why? Why? Why? Why? Why? Why? Why? Why? Why? Why? Why? Why? Why? Why? Why? Why? Why? Why? Why? Why? Why? Why? Why? Why? Why? Why?

"Listen." His voice felt so close, I hadn't realized I had closed my eyes until I opened them and found his. I couldn't breathe. "I know we just met a few days ago. I mean, we haven't even met-met yet. But I..." He paused, searching for the right words. Was this really happening? Finally? "Fuck, why is this so hard?"

"Jasper, I—"

"I can do it, okay? Just give me a second." He pressed his hands against his cheeks and took a deep breath. "These are not just coincidences, and even if they were, I wouldn't give a fuck." He started fidgeting. I kept holding my breath in case an exhale would scare him away. "I can't stop thinking about you, I can't bear not being with you. Your face, your voice, the way you pull at your top lip when you're nervous. I can't. Chiara I... I..."

He stopped talking when his lips grazed mine.

The entire dreamland stopped in its tracks.

It was everything I had imagined and more. Like drinking from a forbidden fountain, the bitter taste of his lips with the paperlike smell of his breath.

He held on to me with the desperation of someone who was about to die.

Deep within myself, I knew it was wrong, that I was condemning him to whatever horrifying future awaited me.

But I was selfish.

And his hands traced my waist in a way that made me feel like an artpiece.

A sculpture.

Something worth fighting for.

An electric current coursed through my body, igniting every nerve ending. Slowly, the kiss deepened, and I lost track of time that never existed in the first place.

I couldn't stop, didn't want to stop. Afraid that it would mean the end.

That I wouldn't be able to feel those lips again. It was like I had finally found my place in the world and all the pieces were falling into place.

So I held onto him, too. Clung to his hair, prepared to rip it away if someone tried to separate us again.

But no shadows came.

Eventually, we had to catch our breath.

"Tell me everything you remember about yourself," he whispered into my teeth. I melted in his chest. "I'll find you, Chiara. I don't know how, but I will."

"The bus. Number 12. It has to mean something." My head started to hurt again. "I take it every day to work and then home. That's the route that changed, but it's the same one."

He shifted uncomfortably and his breathing became agitated.

"I'm waking up. I can feel it." He kissed me again. And again. And again. "Bus 12. That new route. I'll find you. I swear I will. Chiara, I..."

His last word dissolved with him.

The air started growing cold again.

15
Jolted to Reality

I was a fucking idiot.

I didn't even ask for her last name.

Fuck work. Fuck Mondays. I called out because what else was I supposed to do?

I couldn't pretend that life could go on as normal when my entire world was imploding. When she needed my help.

She needed me to find her.

And I hadn't even asked for her fucking last name.

Of course, scouring the internet for hours didn't amount to anything; there were probably a million Chiaras in the world. With my luck, she wouldn't even have any accounts using her actual name.

It was idiotic, impossible.

But I had to do it.

For her.

For her freckles.

For her lips.

For the way her hands clung desperately to my hair, refusing to let go.

I got out of the apartment in a haze, put my phone in Do Not Disturb, and started walking around aimlessly. Like a madman.

What did I have?

The general idea of the area where she lived.

The bus number twelve.

A route she swore she took.

Her name.

Her face.

There had to be something else, something hidden beneath the folds of my brain that maybe, if I dug hard enough, I could find. All the puzzle pieces had to lead somewhere. All the connections, all the times we almost crossed paths but didn't.

I grabbed my phone to check the bus schedule- three missed calls.

From Leo.

Funny, how I would have died a week ago if that had happened.

Funny, how a work crush could turn into nothingness when you find your person.

Was that what Chiara was for me?

My person?

I closed my eyes for a second, just to try to conjure her fragrance in my nostrils one more time.

Earthy. Fresh. Beautiful.

"Excuse me." A man's voice cut through the memory like a poisoned dagger. "Do you know when the next bus is coming?"

"In about ten minutes," I responded, defeated.

"The forty-two, right?" He asked. I nodded. He sat in silence next to me.

It was crazy how everything could go on as normal when my entire world was imploding. And all I had to do at that moment was wait.

Wait for another bus without her in it.

I walked up to the gas station next to the stop and wished with all my might to find any of the things we had seen in our dream. Back when we had barely met.

Was that our first date?

It wasn't like we had known each other for a long time anyway.

But what was time when you were dealing with dreams?

No secret doors leading to haunted basements. To ancient products discontinued a lifetime ago. No candies to remind me of my childhood. No redhead jumping from behind the shelves to show me something she had found.

I grabbed whatever drink I could put my hands on and looked at my phone again, scrolling for no reason in particular. An awful habit, a desperate attempt to numb my brain from the pain of the emptiness she caused.

"Look into my eyes, and tell me what you feel." A pink-haired girl mocked me from the screen. *"For moments like these, falling drops are enough."* Her voice was thick, like molasses.

Of course, the universe would play a trick like that. Show me the song that had reunited us when it meant nothing, when I couldn't do anything to find her.

"Just that?" the attendant asked. I nodded and left my phone on the counter to get my wallet.

The video kept playing.

"Remember to pre-order the Mist Water! The song comes out this Friday!" The thick voice with pink strands said.

But it couldn't be. It was an old song, I knew the entire thing.

I had heard it again and again while looking for Chiara. I knew the lyrics, and she did too.

A song that hadn't been released.

A bus route that wasn't active yet.

A girl who couldn't wake up.

It all had to be connected,

like us.

It had to mean something.

Time was running out, and every time I tried to think about her face, it became distorted again. Sunken, hazy eyes. A smile that showed everything but happiness. An expression of pain. The look of someone who would soon disappear.

It was probably the stupidest plan ever, but I wasn't particularly smart, and I had nothing else to do.

So eventually the bus came, and I made my way to the area where she supposedly lived. A long shot, but maybe since fate had seemed to bring us together, I would have a stroke of luck.

Of course, the universe itself seemed to be pulling us apart as well.

The forty-two became the six.

The six finally took me to the twelve.

I bought a couple of snacks along the way. I had my notebook, some headphones, and the power bank in my backpack. Things to keep me alive, barely. I was wearing my jacket again, the one we had lost in what it almost felt like another life.

It reminded me of her.

The rest of my day was going to be spent on wheels.

Idiotic.

But the best I could come up with.

Every single time we stopped, I looked up to check who would come in, who would get out. I tried to conjure the color of her hair shining between the seats. I would jerk my head to the front every time the door opened, just to go back to whatever I was trying to keep my mind occupied with next.

I lost track of time.

Ran out of ideas on what to doodle

Got carsick when trying to read more than 50 pages of a book on my phone.

Door opened.

Nothing.

Door closed.

No sign of her.

Door opened.

My heart slowly deflated.

Door closed.

My muscles burned in pain.

Door opened.

The driver started to grow suspicious that something was up. He kept eyeing me through the rearview mirror.

Door closed.

Wasn't he supposed to have his eyes on the road?

Door opened.

More people coming in, coming out.

A woman with a baby.

A guy with a student ID.

A redhead with short, messy hair and tired eyes.

Her.

Her.

It was her!

I had to force my hand to cover my mouth just to not scream her name.

Chiara looked exhausted, with deep bags under her eyes and her makeup smudged. Her spark was gone, stolen by whatever monster was trying to catch her now.

She walked towards me, looking at the ground.

I smiled, ready to embrace her, to let her know everything was going to be okay.

We had found each other, and whatever the hell was happening, we would figure it out together.

But our eyes met, and she didn't jump into my arms.

Didn't say my name.

Barely even acknowledged me before sitting down in the row in front of me.

"Hey," I said, leaning to the front, my voice shook a little.

She jumped like an electric shock had coursed all over her body. She stared at me for three seconds too long and then passed her hand quickly through her hair in an attempt to brush it.

"Hi?" she responded with a confused frown.

My stomach sank.

I wanted to throw up.

"Do you... recognize me?" I asked, pretending I wasn't actively dying inside.

The pain of her stare was too much to bear. Like I was a stranger, a nobody. Like we weren't connected. Like we accidentally hadn't spent our entire lives looking for each other without knowing so.

"Should I?" she asked in a flat tone and gave me a polite smile, leaning just a little bit away from me.

"We've met before," I said, trying to make her react. What kind of cruel joke was this?! "My name is Jasper."

The silence between us was deafening, even though the bus was full of people breathing, talking, and living. The world was just the space between us.

The nothingness in her stare.

What the fuck was I supposed to say next?

That we met in a dream?

That we kissed and fell in love in a world that didn't exist?

"Oh, I'm so sorry, my memory is trash." She forced a smile that never reached her eyes. "Did we go to school together?"

Fuck.

Fuck. Fuck. Fuck. Fuck. Fuck.

"Yeah, but I was a couple of years ahead of you," I lied. "No worries. I just recognized you and thought I could say hi."

I needed to get out of there.

"Well, hi!" Her smile looked more authentic that time, but still cold. "Do you take this bus often? I do, but I haven't seen you here before."

"This was a one-time thing," I said, feeling completely defeated.

The bus stopped.

I waved my hand.

I got off.

Was I actually insane?

Was there any world in which I had imagined the whole thing?

It couldn't be, it was impossible. How would I have known she was going to be in that bus?

Now I was on the other side of the city and would need to take at least two buses to get home. All for nothing. She was perfectly fine.

Without me.

I sat down on the curb like the sidekick in a pretty bad movie and ordered a ride through the first app I found. It would hurt my wallet and my stomach, but I couldn't exist. I couldn't think. I couldn't breathe.

Everything we lived through was so real to me, every single detail matched so perfectly together. It had to be real. It *was* real!

But the clues didn't make sense.

A song that hadn't been released.
A bus route that wasn't active yet.
A girl who couldn't recognize me.

What if...?
Is time...?
Are we...?

The thought was too absurd to even think out loud, but the situation itself had exceeded the limits of all logic to begin with.

I couldn't stop toying with the idea until I got to my apartment, until I saw myself in the mirror and noticed the messy hairs growing on my chin, until the eyebags under my eyes screamed at me.

She remembered things that hadn't happened yet.
Because they had already happened for her.

Bile rose from my stomach the second after I kneeled in front of the toilet. The snacks and couple of sips I had the whole day came back, burning from the inside.

It couldn't be fucking real.

And yet, there we were.

Think. Think. Think.

She was awake today, but she can't wake up in our dreams. Something happened that made it so. Something. Something that would cause her pain on her side. Something, maybe while she was listening to that song. Something to make her look like she was losing life. Something with blood.

Something that hadn't happened yet?

"Oh please. I need to know. What the fuck is happening?!" I prayed to no one, because I never got into deity worship.

Fucking useless.

Praying to the void while kneeling on the bathroom rug.

I had found her, and that didn't change anything.

With all the strength I could muster, I dragged myself to my backpack to get the notebook, then to bed.

What were all the clues again?

A song that hadn't been released.

A bus route that wasn't active yet.

She had mentioned a café where she would work sometimes, right before the comment about the bus route. Had she ever told me the name?

A song that hadn't been released.

A bus route that wasn't active yet.

A café I didn't know.

The city came back to my mind. Its purple sky and radioactive stars. The empty buildings. The rundown walls with encrusted clocks. Clocks that had stopped for her, but were ticking for me.

What was the time again?

A song that hadn't been released.

A bus route that wasn't active yet.

A café I didn't know.

Clocks stopped at six forty-two.

That first bus. The way she had found all the trinkets. How she was sure there had been people there before us. A receipt, a hairpin, paper clips, things left behind that probably only meant something to their owner.

Left behind by someone who wasn't there anymore.

Was that what was happening to her?

Would she disappear and leave a bracelet behind for another unfortunate soul to find?

My hand hurt, my mouth was on fire. I could barely move, barely breathe. The clocks were ticking, I could almost hear them reverberating against the walls of my skull. Whatever this was, I couldn't do it alone.

"I will find Chiara in my dreams tonight."

16
Crossing Over

The taste of his lips lingered on my tongue long after he left.

The way his eyes sparkled when he looked at me, like I was a mystery he wanted to drown in.

The quiet rumble of his chest pressed against mine. His heart beating so fast it could have swallowed me whole.

I only opened my eyes when the air grew too cold to bear, wishing he was still there, that my mind had been playing tricks.

The place was desolate, like my soul.

My eyes felt heavy and breathing started feeling like a nightmare. I had slept in Jasper's version of the bus when we were together and that had been fine, but this time felt different.

I tried to get up, but my legs faltered.

Blink.

Maybe I could wait for him there. He had found me once, he would do it again. He had sworn he would help, he would find a way. And my eyelashes were almost stuck together.

Blink.

If only I could have control of that dreamland the same way he had. If I could call upon a bus with pink trim and paperlike wheels. A paper airplane to take me away from there. If only I could be less tired.

Blink.

A rhythmic sound caught my attention, barely. The murmur of a crowd in a world far from here. Something dark crossed the barrier in front of me. A silhouette dragging yellow tubes and rainbow tiles.

Blink.

There they were, just like they had always been. For a second, the familiarity of the shadows made me feel like a child tucked away in bed. They smelled like copper. Rusty. Dangerous.

Bli—

No!

I forced my legs to sustain my weight and used the wall to get up. I couldn't fall asleep, I couldn't give up. Not when Jasper was trying to do as much as he could so we could have a chance together.

I couldn't give up until we kissed again.

I started walking slowly, pretending I didn't see the shadows, trying to keep a steady pace. Forever ago I had read somewhere that if you were afraid and started running, you would let fear take control.

The memory came with a sting in my forehead, like it had almost been plucked away from my brain.

How old had I been?

My brain was working backwards. What would happen when it reached the end?

When there were no more memories to take?

A cold energy shook me from head to toe. I knew, without having to turn around, that the shadows were getting closer and closer. They didn't have to hurry; it was as if they knew they had all the time in the world, because I was running out of mine.

But I had to keep going.

They began to appear in front of me, just a few steps away. A sound of static, a low but forceful murmur reverberated from each one. As I walked, the airport transformed more and more. The ceiling began to lower little by little, and with it, the air began to escape from my lungs.

The shadows continued to approach slowly, the colored tiles on the floor coming loose as they passed over them. Little by little, they joined together into a sinuous figure that rattled with each of my steps.

A multi-colored snake, hissing at me, growing by the second.

Maybe running wouldn't be such a bad idea after all.

I took a deep breath and took a step forward, then another, and another, a little faster each time. Until I was running as fast as I did when I fled from the bus.

But every time I increased my speed, the snake did the same. Its black, forked tongue probed the air beside me.

Until I felt its rough texture brush against one of my wrists.

Until one of the shadows grabbed my ankle.

Until my forehead hit the ground.

I tried to cry but my eyes were dry as the freezing grasp of the shadows pierced my senses. The darkness grew thicker and thicker around me, suffocating me until there was nothing left but the all-consuming void.

I closed my eyes, surrendering to the darkness that had been chasing me for so long.

Tired of running, tired of fighting.

More flashbacks, more disorderly thoughts that wanted to make sense but really didn't.

Couldn't.

I had disappointed Jasper. Everything we had gone through together was for nothing.

I gave up.

A failure.

The void was suffocating, the darkness grew cold until there was nothing else left but my bones. Until the thoughts were no more than a tangled mess of flashes and colors.

Until I opened my eyes again and the shadows were gone.

The monstrous snake had disappeared.

Trees had replaced the concrete walls. Pure white trees, tall and skinny, reaching up to the sky with no leaves on their branches.

They seemed ancient, eternal, immortal.

The air itself seemed devoid of color, of life. A thin mist made silhouettes blurry. The dead forest that surrounded me only shone in greyscale. The sky above was dark and gloomy, like a perpetual storm was coming but never arriving.

I felt less tired, weightless.

Nothing hurt anymore.

Because I couldn't feel anything at all.

Something moved in the tree in front of me.

Something in the bark.

An insect?

I walked toward it, the lines on the trunk looked like symbols I wouldn't have been able to understand even if I had tried.

One of them expanded and contracted.

It couldn't be.

A gleaming white eye, with two lines instead of pupils, stared intently at me. No, not ordinary lines. Clock hands, pointing to the time I was already used to seeing everywhere.

The eye blinked a couple of times before closing completely.

Another eye blinked open just above it.

More eyes opened and closed on the bark of all the trees surrounding me.

I waited for the shiver running down my spine but nothing happened.

Because I couldn't feel anything at all.

I started walking without any specific place to go, just so I wouldn't have to see those eyes judging me.

The silence was deafening, broken only by the sound of my footsteps on the forest floor. Each step seemed to echo through the trees, a reminder that I was completely alone once again.

Only dirt and branches.

Devoid of color.

Devoid of life.

The only source of light came from the glowing wood that surrounded me, bouncing off the mist. I walked for what felt like hours, days. The minutes seemed to stretch into eternity. Nothing hurt anymore, not even my side. And yet, my chest felt empty, something was missing.

One foot in front of the other, waiting for something to happen.

The eyes popping in and out of existence whenever I came closer to each tree.

Something on the floor caught my attention, movement that seemed as strange being in that place as I did. I kneeled down and dug in the dirt. There was something there.

It was calling me.

A pull?

It moved like a worm, I dug until my nails started bleeding, but still didn't hurt. Nothing did anymore.

The black dirt was covering a thin, long root. I pulled on it and more of it began uncovering.

And more.

And more.

Until I reached the first tree, and it kept going.

Like a rope, trying to bring me somewhere, somehow. The pull kept pressing in between my temples, begging me to follow it.

It was a web of thin roots interconnecting every single tree around me, I tugged on them like a spider trying to feel for its prey. One of them started vibrating, glowing at a different frequency than the trees.

I followed it until I was in a clearing engulfed in darkness but kept tugging. Just a bit more.

And more.

And more.

The ground opened below me and I plummeted down. Faster and faster, screaming until my lungs stung. Felt the wind rushing towards my face, drying out my eyeballs. As if the very air around me was conspiring to suffocate me.

Until even the air was gone.

I landed in a saltwater pond that might as well have been made from my own tears. Then, the pain restarted.

The emptiness I had felt in the forest gave way to a stinging, excruciating sensation that rippled from one of my ribs to the rest of my body. I swam up, feeling how my lungs started filling with liquid.

Taking a breath stung almost as much, but finally the numbness had gone away.

I had never imagined how much my brain would miss pain, the feeling of being alive. My eyes got so watery I could barely see a thing.

Oh God, how much I had missed colors.

Pinks and purples painted the sky like watercolors, a calm garden with millions of flowers surrounded the lake I was now in the middle of. The pain started calming down, at least enough to let me swim to the shore.

I felt fine, finally.

A good, simple calm. The pain gradually faded into the background, and the flowers by the lake distracted me enough that I didn't have to think about it.

I knelt down to smell one of them and its fragrance traveled through my nerves.

A smile appeared on my face.

Peace.

A peace I had only felt once before. Peace accompanied by a song I recognized well enough.

It told me that everything would be okay.

Everything would be okay, just like when I put on the headphones after finding them for the first time.

The headphones.

Calm.

Finally.

"You look like a corpse!" The memory of Jasper's words echoed inside my head.

No!

I plucked the flower with both hands, letting out a scream that faded with the wind. It screeched with me, inside my head.

I was back at work, practicing my smile in the bathroom mirror, trying to make sure the apron was tied just a bit too tight around my waist.

With a blink, I got back to the garden, to the screaming flower that was now wilting in between my fingers, becoming dark and grey like the dirt that still clung to my nails.

I plucked another one, another screech. And another one. And another one.

Each was accompanied by an irrelevant memory that stung my forehead like bees. Almost like my life was flashing before my eyes.

But there had to be something there, something I was missing.

A clue, a missing piece.

I got to another flower, this one harder to pluck than the rest. It bit me, but I kept going, and pulling, and pulling.

Until I was back on the bus. The real one, the one I always took.

Bus twelve.

I was exhausted, drained, a day of dealing with people would do that to anyone. At that point, I had already given up on makeup and looking presentable. I just wanted to walk to my seat and dissociate for an hour until I got home.

"Hey." I heard the voice a second after I sat down.

All the hairs on my body stood on end when I heard it. Soft, melodious. Out of this world. I turned around and found the perfect face of a guy with soft, delicate features and black hair. Silver highlights decorated it. He looked impossibly beautiful.

Oh no. No.

That couldn't be happening.

Was I really living my perfect moment I had waited for all my life, without makeup, without a hair brush?!

I ran my hand through my hair in a desperate attempt to look at least a bit nicer.

Had I even brushed my teeth that day at lunch?

"Hi?" I responded and tried to play it cool. Confused, but yearning for something else to happen. Something to take me away from the monotony.

"Do you... recognize me?" He asked with a soft smile.

Did I?

I tried to look inside my brain as much as I possibly could. It couldn't be work, I had literally just left, and I would remember his face. Maybe he worked somewhere I used to frequent? That café I used to stop at halfway home?

Where?

Where could I have possibly seen him?

I would have remembered, for sure. He looked like he didn't belong in reality. I had to know, I had to. I had to.

"Should I?" I asked, still looking inside my memories to no avail. I smiled at him, trying to be as normal about it as I possibly could.

He was close, too close to me. I was inhaling his breath.

It was too much. Too fast. Too close.

I leaned away from him, even just to oxygenate my brain enough, to think clearly.

"We've met before," he said, and I wanted to scream. "My name is Jasper."

I couldn't think, couldn't move. Was it some kind of joke? A terrible pickup line?

"Oh, I'm so sorry, my memory is trash!" I smiled, still trying to pinpoint him. Where? Where?! A bar? A club? School? School! "Did we go to school together?"

That had to be impossible, but what other explanation was there?

People change, I suppose, maybe that was why I didn't have that stare fixated in my mind.

He looked at me, and it was like staring into my soul. He smiled as if he knew me, deeply, intimately.

"Yeah, but I was a couple of years ahead of you," he said simply, and something in his expression changed. "No worries. I just recognized you and thought I could say hi."

That was it?

I had to do something, say something. It was probably the only moment I would have for something actually interesting happening to me.

"Well, hi!" I smiled and hoped it didn't seem too big, too weird. "Do you take this bus often? I do, but I haven't seen you here before."

Maybe we'll have a bit of time. We could start talking and find out all the things we had in common. Maybe he'd like me enough to ask for my number; maybe I'd do the same.

His smile disappeared in a second.

Did I do something wrong?

"This was a one-time thing," he whispered and sat back again.

The memory faded, and I was back at the garden.

He looked full of life, excitement, joy. I licked my lips, remembering the feeling of his. That day, his face was perfectly shaven, smooth. His eyes were filled with light, and he looked rested, happy. Unlike the uneven beard hairs that had started to grow on his chin last time we saw each other, decorated by eye bags filled with stress.

He remembered me that day, even though I had never seen him before.

Time was playing a trick on us.

We were out of sync.

The realization hit me so hard I got dizzy and grabbed the first thing I could see. Another flower, another memory.

Same bus, a different day.

A song that had just been released.

Stabbing pain in my side.

17
Joyful Eden

Eighty-five
Eighty-six

I counted the steps in the spiral staircase, forcing myself to slow down and my heart to beat at a steady pace. Even though deep down a part of me was crying and screaming in desperation, that wasn't how things worked.

Ninety-two

Slow and steady, I had almost reached the top. Something itched. My toe? I ignored it, told my brain it wasn't there. My body was already immobile, asleep. Scratching it now would throw away all my efforts. I focused on my breath.

Just a bit more

Ninety-nine

The end of the climb welcomed me with a white door, I visualized it glowing a bit brighter than usual. I needed it to work; I could use all the help I could possibly get.

I had promised myself to never go back to the Waiting Room; it led to too many possibilities, provided too much control. The power of being able to construct my dreams so carefully had almost been the death of me.

I guess having downed that entire bottle of sleeping aid liquid hadn't helped.

But the bus wasn't enough. I couldn't trust it to take me in the right direction. I couldn't wait for some magical headphones to appear in Chiara's hands again, to have her be the one doing all the work, leading me to her.

The door opened and I took a deep breath, detaching more and more from my body and focusing on the senses that didn't really exist.

I saw the white walls around me. Bare, a blank canvas perfect for any of my desires. They had been waiting for me for years since the last time I tried to replace my reality with dreams.

I felt their smooth texture, polished like marble. Made sure to run each of my fingers over it, to trick my brain into believing it was real. It wasn't difficult; I was already used to it.

I listened to the silence and beneath it, white noise. Like ants trying to get into my ears, it was the perfect foundation for any atmosphere I wanted to create.

I tasted the plain water from a glass on a white table and concentrated on the coldness of the liquid as it ran down my throat.

I smelled everything, and nothing at the same time. The scent of air conditioning in an empty office. Of cleanliness. Of disinfectant. The closest thing my brain could recognize to the absence of smell.

"Chiara," I said out loud without moving my lips. "Where are you now?"

The smell was the first sense I caught that time, her essence slowly reaching from the part of our brains that were connected in ways none of us would ever comprehend.

Flowers. Marigolds?

I tasted blood, and my heart dropped. The Waiting Room started shaking, and I took another deep breath to stabilize it.

I guess I was a bit out of practice after all.

I listened for any sound that could give me an indication of her. Her voice, her breath. Distant, barely distinguishable sobbing came through my ears.

Don't react.

Not yet.

I moved my fingers and tried to feel something in the empty space between them. Drops of liquid coagulated against the bed of my nails.

I was getting closer.

I closed my eyes and took a deep breath. When I opened them, the Waiting Room had completely transformed.

The walls look like they would have been colorful forever ago, but the paint had peeled off and darkened. The furniture was thrown around, pieces of crumbled paper accumulated in mountains against the corners. Scratches on the floor. Plushies that had been stepped on and ripped open. Picture frames with nothing in them.

Was this how her brain looked?

Lying on the floor, a phone flashed the screen on and off. I walked towards it and extended my hand, my intuition imploring me to stop digging, but my heart begging me to keep going.

The second I grabbed it, the room shook like an earthquake, and cracks started appearing on the floor.

"Give me that!" The scream of a man, muffled behind music, reverberated all around.

Not any ordinary music.

The song.

The one Chiara had been listening to.

The phone grew hot, scalding, but I kept holding to it as if my life depended on it. I had a feeling hers might have.

"Are you fucking deaf?!" The voice screamed behind the lyrics.

Water began to fill the room, slowly seeping through cracks that were starting to break the walls apart.

The water rose up, and up, and up.

Until everything was darkness, and the phone dissolved against my palm. I floated up. Maybe I was drowning in real life. Maybe something had gone wrong, and my actual apartment was flooding. Maybe I was sleeping with my mouth open and a bug was creeping into my throat at the exact moment.

I floated up, waiting to hit the ceiling, but instead a purple sky welcomed me.

And screams, different ones this time.

"Jasper?!" Her voice was hoarse and broken, like a radio about to have its batteries replaced.

The salt burned my eyes, but I didn't care. Swimming to shore, I opened my arms, and she threw herself into them. "Oh, Jasper, you came. You came! You found me!"

She felt dangerously weightless, like she would break in half if I hugged her too tightly.

I kissed her face until I couldn't breathe anymore. Every single one of her freckles, her tears. Her lips were dried up and chapped, broken.

"I saw you, but you didn't... You didn't recognize me, and I was..." Speaking was painful; taking a second away from her skin to speak seemed like torture. "I was so scared I imagined this... And you weren't real... And I..."

"I remember now!" She cried against my lips. "You didn't have a beard. That's how I realized."

Her fingers navigated from my neck to my chin and caressed the stubble on my chin. I nodded to let her know I understood.

Time had been playing a trick on us, or helping us, or maybe both.

"All the pieces are coming together," I said while we slowly started melting towards the floor. "All of them but one." I supported my weight with my elbow when we lay down and hovered my hand next to her side, too afraid that touching her was crossing a line we never had time to establish. "What's causing the pain on your side?"

Her eyes filled with tears, and her lips trembled. She ran her fingers down my arm until they reached my hand, and pressed it against her skin softly.

She took a deep breath and pointed at a section of the garden that was different from the rest. The flowers there were wilted, black. The floor turned into a dark, gooey substance.

"I think they're my memories, somehow," she explained in a barely audible whisper. "Plucking them hurt, but they helped me remember."

"Like the headphones?" I asked, she nodded.

"Something happened inside the bus, that same one we met at. I had my headphones and was playing a stupid game on my phone, so I didn't notice at first." She started, taking a breath to catch her tears. I wiped them with a kiss and held her tight. "A man started screaming at me and tried to grab my phone, and I didn't know what to do! Because I need it. You know? My life is in there. Why would he just grab it like that?! I don't know. Reflexes kicked in, I guess? I pulled back. And the song kept playing. I had it on loop because it had just been released, and I was excited. I saw it all around on social media, and it's so nice. Did you know the artist started doing concerts on her pickup truck? She's..."

"Chiara, please." I pleaded and grabbed her chin. "What did the man do to you?"

"I don't know. So much pain. Piercing. Oh, Jasper, it's the worst pain I've felt in my life," she was crying again. I held her close to my chest. "I think he stabbed me, and I dropped my stupid phone, and I think I hit my head because everything turned dark and people were screaming and the song was still playing in the FUCKING HEADPHONES BECAUSE IT WAS ON LOOP. JASPER, I'M GOING TO DIE! I'M GOING TO DIE BECAUSE OF MY STUPID PHONE. I'M DYING, JASPER. I'M FUCKING DYING. I DON'T WANT TO DIE!"

Her tears mixed with mine. I hugged her with all the strength I could muster at that moment. The strength of feelings I was just beginning to understand. The strength of the desperation I felt at that moment, because

I didn't know how to help her.

The flowers around us began to grow taller and taller. Perhaps it was her brain's way of protecting the precious seconds we had left.

Together.

Her lips sought mine desperately, and I let her drink the last of my strength. Sweet and bitter.

Like us.

Her silhouette began to intertwine with mine. I took strands of her hair and began to kiss them as if it were the last time I would see them, while her hands ran down my neck.

She was a poem so deep and volatile that no one in the world could write. Her eyes looked at me like no one had ever done so before. Her legs were clinging to me as if I was about to disappear.

I took her in my arms and kissed every inch of her skin, whispering unintelligible words against the freckles on her shoulders. I exhaled all the life I could offer against her side, in a ridiculous attempt to heal a wound that neither of us could see.

It was as if nothing else in the world existed, and in a way, that was true.

We were lost in each other, consumed by the uncertainty the universe had thrown us into. But we fit against each other so perfectly. Everything had led to this.

To us.

"I won't let you die," I whispered against her chest. "I don't know how, but I won't."

18
Critical Clues

The way his fingers brushed my skin so delicately.

The softness of his voice whispering that everything would be okay.

The warmth of his lips.

They were all fragments of a perfect dream, our dream. We defeated the universe for a moment; we made that horrific nightmare a paradise.

For a minute, not even the tears dared to interrupt us.

For a second, we were free.

It lasted forever, but eventually ended, as all good things do.

Despair got stuck in my throat. I hid my face in Jasper's chest for as long as I could, as if he couldn't feel me shivering, breaking down again. His hands trembled too; he had sworn he wouldn't let me die.

How could he be so stupid?

How could he make a promise he didn't know if he could keep?

Still pretending I was fine, I ran the tips of my fingers over his chest. Maybe I could memorize every single one of his pores; that sounded like a nice last memory to have.

My fingers came closer to his scars, glistening beneath the pink and purple hues of light bouncing between the clouds. Tiny stars speckled the firmament like watercolor, splashed.

"They're nice, right?" He asked with a smile, and his voice broke down a little bit. "Very proud of how they healed."

We were both trying to keep up the act a little longer. To pretend reality wasn't going to come crashing down any moment.

"They're shining," I whispered, tracing them with the point of my index finger. "It's so beautiful."

He was angelic, ethereal.

He was heaven.

"So many people swear by fancy creams and miracle remedies. Wanna know my secret?" His hand found my face, and he slightly pulled it up, just so I could see his. "Tons of rest, literally just lying in bed and letting them heal on their own."

His laugh was so unexpected that I couldn't help but imitate him.

It was absurd, beautiful.

Extraordinary.

A good last memory to have.

I laughed so hard my cheeks hurt, and the sides of my mouth started cracking. My chest constricted as I tried to steady my breathing. It was a good belly laugh, one of the ones that escape you without being able to control them. The ones that make you snort and move side to side. The ones that mess with your balance until you fall down to the floor and can't help but roll around. The ones that make your nose runny and your eyes watery.

And my eyes were so watery.

Tears.

Tears coming and going.

Tears.

So many tears.

Until the laugh dissipated,

but the tears remained.

"Thank you," I whispered with a voice that broke down into a million pieces.

"You can thank me when you wake up," he responded with a desperation that broke my heart.

"What if it can't be helped?" It hurt, saying it out loud. The tears burned my freckles away. "What if we were put here together just so you could bid me farewell?"

All the blood in his body came to his face. It turned bright red, his eyes just about to pop out, his veins vibrating underneath his skin.

"Don't. You. Dare." I would have preferred him to scream, to get upset at me. To do anything other than see me with that pain, that despair. "We'll figure this out together. I don't give a fuck how. I'm not giving up and you aren't either!"

Even then, his voice stayed firm, but soft.

He kissed me one, two, three times. His tears healed what mine had burned.

I didn't deserve him.

I was too impulsive, too explosive.

I felt too much too quickly, then burned out on people like my life depended on it.

I was too emotional and a robot without emotions.

I was too boring, too normal, too simple, too extra.

Too easy.

Too annoying.

Too closed off.

Too vain.

Too disheveled.

"There's so much for us to do, so many places to visit." He said. His lips were barely moving, pressed against my skin. "You can't die because we have to go on a real date, and do normal people things like complain about our jobs, not run away from monsters and shadows."

"Fuck normal people," I responded with a smile. And with that, all the doubts left my mind.

"Yes! Fuck them!" He smiled as well, hugged me one last time, and then leaned back.

There we go. The conversation, the unavoidable part.

He stared at me without rushing me; we both knew exactly what came next. The tension was almost as palpable as the pain, as the bags under our eyes.

"What if I don't remember enough?" I looked down when I said it, almost ashamed.

"Let's try, okay? Just try."

And I tried.

I tried so hard that I started seeing little speckles in my vision.

Nothing else came to mind, at least nothing other than what I had said already.

He tried to help, of course he did.

"We know about bus twelve, and it has to be happening at six forty-two," he said. "Do you remember something from outside the window? Or maybe you can give me your phone number, and I can call you."

"I would freak out, Jasper. It's me from the past. I don't really know you. Honestly, I probably wouldn't even pick up, I hate phone calls." I hugged my knees. Why did it have to be so hard?

"Maybe a text," he was grasping at straws, we both were. I shook my head.

"Why would I pay attention to a random dude's message?" I laughed a bit at the absurdity of the situation, and the pain in my side made me wish I hadn't.

"I mean... Okay, it's a stupid idea, but I don't know what else to do." The panic started leaking through his words again.

But I did know what to do.

I took a deep breath and mustered the courage I didn't even have.

"Please don't get mad at me," I whispered and got up to the nearest flower I could find.

He was too late to stop me before I pulled it.

The memory of my puppy when she first came home flooded my brain. She was so tiny, and her belly was so round that she looked like a pear.

"No!" I heard his voice when I came to.

He didn't have to tell me how I looked; I felt my eyes hurt and my cheeks turning more and more hollow by the minute. He tried to pull me away, but I ripped another flower with me.

More pain.

Now it was the time I had to call 911, because working in retail was miserable, and there were seven people trying to rob our store.

But the voice that came out of my mouth wasn't mine. It sounded incorporeal, like it came from someone else.

Someone else a few seats behind me.

Muffled by a song.

"Someone called 911 already," I whispered in his arms. "Right before the man pulled my phone away. On the bus."

"You have to stop doing that. We can figure it out without you hurting yourself more." He said, his entire body shivering. His hands tried to hold my arms, but he was weak too. The nightmare reality looming over our heads was draining both of our energy.

I nodded, then broke away and held on to another flower.

The bus.

Bus twelve.

I need to know.

Please, I need to know something, anything at all.

I can't give up.

Not when he's believing so much in me.

In us.

There was the man with bloodshot eyes and a maniacal smile. I had looked up for a second, but saw his face too well, felt his spit hitting mine.

In the stupid struggle over my phone, he pushed me until my head hit the window. In the background, the song was accompanied by a woman crying on the phone, calling emergency services. I got so dizzy.

So, so dizzy.

The window.

What was in the window?

The memory began to fade into pure fog. I lost my balance back in the dream, back with him. But instead of hitting the ground, Jasper's arms held me safe.

It couldn't end, not yet.

The window. I had to focus.

The window.

I closed my eyes and felt myself slowly losing strength, consciousness. But the scene appeared before me again.

A stop sign. A traffic light.

An intersection.

Letters.

What did the letters say?

My head hurt too. How didn't I remember that? Something warm, wetting my hair. Had I bitten my tongue too? I could smell how it tasted, colors faded. Things stopped making sense. Sounds. Images danced, danced around. Fading.

I was leaving again, but no, no. I couldn't leave.

Almost there.

A little more, just a little more.

I had to do it.

For us.

It was the pain in my side that finally made me drop the phone.

Stupid phone.

I hated it now.

I doubled over. The scream that came out of my mouth didn't feel like mine; it was that of a wild animal, cornered, about to die.

I screamed. I screamed as loud as I could.

The pain was overwhelming.

The window.

The intersection.
What street was it?

"Parkview." The word came out of my mouth without me realizing it. "And... main? Traffic light. Stop sign."

The memory kicked me out with an electric shock, and we both fell to the ground this time. I could barely move my arms around his neck; he lay with me, caressing my face.

"Six forty-two. Parkview and Main Street. Bus twelve," he repeated to himself. Again, and again, and again. "When?"

"The song. That day. It was new, that's why it was on loop." The words began to flow without my control from my delirious lips. "I do that. New song. Songs on loop. I like—I like knowing the lyrics. Music is nice. Do you like music, Jasper?"

It was so difficult to string my thoughts together. I could hear my voice cracking and breaking into incomplete sounds.

Everything was so bright.

The sky, the clouds, the stars, the silver streaks in Jasper's hair.

Jasper.

Beautiful Jasper.
The most beautiful man in the world.

"I promised you, remember?" He was trying so hard to speak calmly, but his voice betrayed him. "I promised you I wouldn't let anything happen to you. And I'm going to keep that promise, okay?"

He set my head down on the ground with the delicacy of someone handling the most precious treasure in history.

The ground was so, so comfortable.

The entire world was spinning around.

But we weren't even in the world anymore.

Spinning.
Spinning.
Spinning.

"Please hold on, Chiara. Please," he asked me, begged me.

"Hold on, Chiara," I repeated. "Hold on. Hold on."

His hands were becoming less and less tangible.

"Trust me. I promise." his voice was fading too. "Just hang in there, okay? I love you, Chiara. See you soon, okay?"

"I love you, Chiara." My brain couldn't conjure sentences on its own.

"I love you. I love you. I love you."

A little laugh escaped my lips.

It was completely nonsensical, loving someone without ever having met them.

But what a beautiful last memory it would be.

19
Jumpstart

I stared at the computer screen for longer than I thought it was possible, the blue light trying to burn my corneas.

How dare life move on?

How could I keep pretending to be alive when I didn't know if she would survive?

Eating was irrelevant, resting, existing. The only thing worth it was thinking. Thinking about her, about how to help. How to survive this mess.

I left work, headed home. Barely touched my phone.

I should have pressed her to give me her number.

But it wouldn't have worked, she knew herself better than I did.

A nap, maybe if I took a nap, I could visit her. Try to stretch that moment infinitely.

That perfect moment kept repeating itself over and over in my brain.

All the counting to one hundred, all the stairs, all the visualizations amounted to the same thing.

Pure darkness.

Two hours passed, three, four? Spent in a hazy blur between being asleep and awake. My stomach growled, and I silenced it with reheated leftovers.

How dare life move on?

A cold shower only put me in a worse mood, woke me up more, reminded me of how warm she felt and how soft her skin was. Not even the water could drown out my screams.

I lay down again, my brain too active to calm down. It was hopeless, I was useless, a failure. Chiara was going to die because I was useless and didn't know how the fuck to help her.

I tried to go over all the clues.

It was impossible to concentrate.

I picked up my phone and checked the singer's profile who was going to release the song. I needed to be sure, to have all the details right.

Friday. I had until Friday.

I had time; everything was going to be fine. I just needed to figure everything out before that time. I got it, I got it.

A song that hadn't been released.
A bus route that wasn't active yet.
A café I didn't know.
Clocks stopped at six forty-two.
A traffic light.
An intersection: Parkview and Main Street.

I drank the rest of the sleep aid I had left and smiled. I just needed to see her again, to make sure she was okay. That her weakness when I dissolved had been temporary, that she had been able to open her eyes after resting. That she was still in that starry garden, looking at the stars.

I opened my eyes again, in total darkness.

Early morning.

A night without dreams.

Two hours passed, five, seven?

I stared at the computer screen for longer than I thought it was possible, the blue light trying to burn my corneas.

How dare life move on?

I left work, headed home. Couldn't nap this time. Couldn't do anything useful.

I was useless, a failure.

A plan, I needed a plan. It was two days away; I still had time. Things could still work out.

I got it. I got it.

According to the digital map on my laptop's screen, there was a business in the exact intersection Chiara had mentioned.

Hidden Garden Bistro.

I could wait there. Be there for her. Wait for the bus to come. Try to help in some way.

But how?

How?

How?

How?

A part of me didn't want to admit I was too afraid of closing my eyes. What if I arrived at that garden again, but Chiara hadn't opened her eyes? What if I was already too late?

What if time had never been on our side after all?

"Ok, that's it. You're telling me what's wrong, dude." Leo's voice made me jump.

How had night turned to day? How could my body dare bring me to work again and pretend life moved on?

The answer came crashing to my senses harder than I anticipated. It was idiotic, unfair.

"I feel like shit, but I already called out Monday," I whispered, covering my face with my hands. He couldn't see me like this. Not like this.

"We've been friends for a while now, Jasper. You know you can tell me if something is wrong." Leo brought his chair next to mine and put a hand on my shoulder.

I couldn't...

I just couldn't hold it any longer.

She was gonna die, and I was useless.

I had spent the whole week in a haze that wouldn't let me breathe.

I had fucked up my life, my dreams, my brain.

The flood of tears was so intense that I had to cover my mouth with my hands to calm the heart-wrenching sounds coming from my throat. Leo stood up for a second, and I heard him lock the door of the small IT office we shared. Then he sat back down next to me and wrapped his arms around me.

He let me cry until I was nothing but a trembling mess. Until I could open my eyes and see him there, silently watching me with concern but without judgment.

"Someone..." I began, but I was afraid that saying it out loud would make it real. I took a deep breath. "Someone I care about... They're not okay, Leo. They're... It's bad. Really bad."

"Hurt?" he asked quietly, as if raising his voice would break me.

"Sick," I lied. Because what the fuck else was I supposed to tell him?

Leo, whom I had always fantasized about going out with, whom I had tried so hard not to interact with in any unprofessional way because it was "wrong." Leo, who now hugged me, held me, told me that everything would be okay.

Leo, who had said we were friends when I thought he barely remembered I existed because we worked together.

"Look, I'm not going to pretend to understand what you're going through right now, but you're not alone." he said calmly, looking me in the eyes. "I know we don't talk much outside of work, but I care about you. You helped me a lot when I started here, and I'll never forget that."

"I just don't know what to do, I feel so useless." My mask had fallen off and cracked, but that was the last thing I cared about. "And working while knowing what's going on is... impossible."

"Look, tomorrow is Friday, and we almost never have urgent tickets." He leaned over and took a box of tissues from the desk, offered them to me, and I thanked him silently. "Stay home, or go visit that person if you can. What does money matter at a time like this?"

"It's complicated, Leo. I don't have a roommate, I pay my rent by myself..." I hated this. I hated my brain, forcing myself to be pragmatic and logical in the absolute worst fucking cases.

"We'll figure it out. I'm probably going to do a shit ton of overtime this week." He hugged me tightly, a real hug, a hug that said he cared more than I thought. "We're brothers, dude, I've got you."

I still thought about that hug when I got home.

It was a different kind of warmth than I had felt with her. Lighter, more balanced. A brotherly warmth, uncomplicated, simple. Family where I didn't expect to find it. It helped me concentrate when I sat down at my notebook, putting everything else aside and writing down all the ideas I could think of for how to deal with tomorrow.

Something lurked under the surface. One of those ideas, just running through my mind.

I tried to ignore it over and over again.

It was very stupid, too risky.

But was there another option?

That night was also dreamless, and for the first time in a long while, I woke up late the next morning.

I forced myself to eat and drink. I checked out the song released that morning and played it in the background while I got ready to go out. That song.

Our song.

Taking care of myself was the only way I could prepare. Make sure I wouldn't faint because my stomach had been empty for far too long. I couldn't let anything go wrong when the weight of the entire world rested on my shoulders.

My world.

In the afternoon, I took money from savings and ordered a ride to the café; the last thing I wanted at that moment was to get on another bus. Life would get on track after that day, for better or worse.

Half of my brain hated the other at that moment. I told myself over and over again that I had to get on with her, that I had to be there when it all happened.

But what if I got hurt too?

What if I made everything worse by trying to help her?

No.

The option that kept haunting me was still there, in the back of my mind.

It was there at five, when I sat down at the table next to the window. Fidgeting. It was there at six, when I went to the bathroom and threw up because of the nerves.

Time felt wrong, stretched, running almost too slowly. I had spent so much of the last few days between dreaming and wishing I was doing so, that I had started losing grasp of reality again. But things would get on track.

Hopefully with her.

Six thirty

I looked out of the window. The street was bustling happily. No one had any idea. I felt trapped, suffocated. People ran around with smiles and frowns, clueless. Like zombies in the middle of a dreamland. Without feelings, without thoughts.

Six thirty-five

There they were. The traffic light, the stop sign, the street signs at the intersection. And time decided to be slow again, almost painfully, ripping my skin apart. That thought, bothering me still in the back of my brain, made it almost as unbearable as time itself.

Six thirty-nine

I got up, careful not to run. The last thing I needed was to draw weird suspicions that would ruin the moment. My only moment to help her.

I walked to the intersection and pressed the button to cross the street. One time, two times. Three. Four. It was frantic and erratic, but I tried to stay calm.

Six forty-one

The traffic light turned red, and a couple of people crossed the street. I stayed, disregarding their confused stares.

But no, that was wrong.
It was too early.
Too early.
The light turned green again, cars started up again.
Fuck.
Fuck, no.
Fuck. Fuck. Fuck.

Fuck. Fuck.

A blue bus, swerving erratically, approached the intersection. The number on it, barely visible still, mocked me.

Twelve.

Six forty-two.

It came closer, closer, closer.

People screamed at it in confusion, car horns blared.

It was too much, too loud, I couldn't hear my own thoughts fighting against each other.

The idea took control of my body before I could stop it, maybe I wouldn't have even if I had the opportunity.

It was very stupid, too risky.

But probably the only way.

Police sirens joined the chaos of the noise that suffocated my senses.

Only one thing was true in that moment:

that bus can't keep going.

Only one thought filled my mind when I jumped in front of that bus:

I refuse to be useless any longer.

20
Journey to Forever

Total darkness.

All the sounds that a moment ago were crashing around in my brain have been sucked into a deafening void.

Perhaps a second has passed since I began to remember everything that had led me to this point, perhaps even less.

My life flashing before my eyes.

Is this what dying feels like?

Deep down, I knew this was the only way, the result of a stupid experiment that fate had played on us. Her life in exchange for mine.

Chiara.

I hope that at least my sacrifice will be enough.

That I haven't failed her.

I take a deep breath, waiting for it all to end at once.

A high-pitched beep fills my ears for a moment. Darkness starts to dissipate, turning into millions of stars behind my eyelids.

Sounds start coming through again. People screaming, the sirens coming closer and closer. I blink once, twice.

A flash of light too bright. I rub my eyes and slowly my vision adjusts to my surroundings. The bus is stopped a few feet in front of me. The front and rear doors are open, and people rush in and out.

Am I... alive?

"He ran away!" someone shouts, and some pedestrians run in the direction they point. "Watch out! He has a knife!"

A huge commotion, someone pulls me by the arm to get me off the street.

I'm alive!

My whole body is shaking from head to toe. My muscles are stiff, trying to react. It's all too much. Too much. Oh, too fucking much, I can barely breathe. And think. And I can't even move. But maybe... Maybe it wasn't a total failure! Maybe she's good! Safe.

She has to be safe.

Oh, please, please.
Please, whatever's out there.
Please have her be safe.

"Police are coming!" I hear another voice shout from the bus. "There are people bleeding here!"

More people are running off the bus when one bumps into me, and finally, my feet can react. The sirens are getting closer, but they're not here yet.

Is time still working against us?

I run past the front doors of the bus, but the commotion makes it impossible to move inside.

"I called 911, they have to be close!"

I keep hearing voices disconnected from their mouths, because no one else is important in this moment. No one other than her.

Her.

Her.

Her.

Where is she?
Where's Chiara?

I scream her name one, two times. No one responds; someone dares to shush me, and I push them aside. I don't have time to deal with anyone or anything other than her. I need to know she's safe. To know she's okay.

The smell is horrid. Metal, panic, blood. If I hadn't thrown up at the café, I definitely would be doing it here. A woman, I assume the bus driver, is helping someone who's passed out across one of the front seats.

"He started threatening everyone," a teenage boy cried on a phone a couple of seats away from where I was. "He pulled out a knife. No, no. No mom, I'm okay. I'm just... Please, please pick me up. No, I can't move. It's too much."

I agree. Everything is too fucking much. It has been too much the whole day. Fuck, it's been like that since this shitshow started.

"Chiara!" I screamed again, my vocal cords imploring me to calm down.

I push and shove a couple more people out of the way.

Until finally, her face.

Chiara is passed out in between the arms of two strangers, trying to get her out of the bus, away from the commotion. Her face is pale, her hair disheveled and dull. But it's her. It's her with her fishnets and bracelets. It's her, all dressed in black, with smudged eyeliner underneath her eyes. It's her, it's finally her!

I try to come closer, but bump into someone. Again.

Fuck. Fuck. Fuck. Fuck.

"Please! Please, I know her!" I can sense the pain in my voice. "Chiara! Chiara, wake up!"

Something under my foot makes me slip and fall to the ground. I curse loudly and start looking to see what it is. A black earphone, camouflaged against the metal floor. I bring it to my ear, even though I already know exactly what I'm going to find.

A song I already know by heart.

And further away, under another seat, the phone playing it.

"Hey! Hey, he's stealing that phone!" The teenager I saw earlier shouts. I stand up and find him pointing at me.

Someone grabs my wrist, and I use all my strength to break free. The two people carrying Chiara finally manage to get her off the bus, and I lose sight of her face.

It's too much.

The humid air, with sweat particles sticking to my skin. I can't breathe, I can't think. I try to open my mouth to explain that it's a misunderstanding, that I just want to give her back the phone that almost cost her her life.

Almost.

I hope with all my heart that this is the right word.

Amidst the chaos and commotion of the other passengers, I manage to escape the grip of the couple who mistook me for a criminal and finally get off the bus.

She is there, lying on the sidewalk. A group of three or four people is gathered around her, another kneeling beside her, trying to apply pressure to the wound in her side.

The sirens, finally. Here.

More commotion, people speaking loudly, screaming, crying. I can see everything happening in slow motion, time again playing tricks against our hearts.

"Oh, Chiara, Chiara!" I throw myself at her, and the person helping me pulls me away.

"Careful! She lost a lot of blood!" they scold me.

I...

I don't know what to do.

Wasn't this enough?

I stopped the bus. Help is arriving. It has to be enough. Right?

Right?

Right?

Other people talk around me, they deposit someone else on the sidewalk. What the fuck happened? Why are so many hurt?

"Chiara, I got your phone." I press my lips against her forehead and kiss it one, two times. "I got your phone, I got your phone, I got your phone."

I tried to put it on her hand, to close her fingers on it. But she's too weak, too nimble.

"Do you know her?" A man asks, and I nod between tears and snot running down my nose.

"Sir, please step aside," a different voice demands; stern, almost deadly. They pull my arm with just enough pressure to get me away from her, and I scream as if one of my nerves had been split in half.

"No! No, please. Don't take her away, please!" I can't even recognize my own voice. Trembling in a pitch too high to be normal.

She's getting put onto a stretcher, and it's taking my breath away with her. They're taking her away from me like all the shadows and zombies and monsters tried to do. But I can't let them win. I won't, I promised her.

I'll keep my promise.

I will.

I will.

"Let me go with her, please." I manage to stand up, clinging to one of the EMTs that was following the ones who are taking her again. "Please, I need to make sure she's okay. Please. You don't understand. She needs me."

I lie.

I lie because she doesn't need me. She has people helping her, she's being put into an ambulance. She has professionals who can do a million things I'm incapable of doing. People who can actually save her life.

I lie because she doesn't need me,

I need her.

"I know her. Her name is Chiara," I whisper barely audibly.

The man looks at me with a furrowed brow and turns his head towards another one about to board the ambulance, who had stopped to look at our exchange. He's holding something in his hand. A thick rectangle with pink and black plushies dangling from it.

Chiara's wallet.

He opens it and looks at it for a few seconds, then at me.

Do they think I'm lying?

He nods, and the one I was speaking to gives me a pat on the back.

"Just don't be in the way. Okay, kid?"

I make my way inside the ambulance, my heart beating the fastest it has in my entire life. I try to crouch next to her, but someone pushes me aside.

I'm so fucking useless.

I'm useless and too late.

I should have died.

I should have boarded the bus with her.

Minutes pass and I stay crouched in a corner of the ambulance with the doors still open, a flurry of activity I don't understand inside. Tears streaming down my face, the pain now stuck in my throat.

"Please. Please wake up. Please," I whisper to myself, doubting she can hear it.

Shivering, trying to peek at whatever the fuck is happening with her. The strength slowly giving away, my eyes feeling heavier and heavier.

"Please. Please. Please wake up, Chiara. Please"

They're speaking amongst each other, but I can't understand the words. It's a foreign, absurd language that doesn't matter. Because nothing else matters if she's not here. If we can't be together.

What a fucking stupid joke from fate to bring us so close to the end, just to...

"Hey!" The man who let me ride with her takes me out of the spiral I was slowly crawling into.

He just points at her and I immediately throw myself at her side.

Her eyelashes flicker slightly, and I hold her hand. A vague, weak pulse makes me feel alive again.

"Hold on. Hold on." I hear in a faint voice. Her beautiful voice. "I love you, Chiara. I love you, I love you."

"Hey, hey, it's me," I whisper next to her ear, caressing her hair ever so slightly. "I'm here, you're going to be okay."

"Jasper?" Her head turns to see me, her green eyes filled with tears, her lips trembling. "You came."

"I promised," I respond in between cries.

Author's Note

I wrote this book at a very weird time of my life. For a long time, I believed I could only write from pain, that I had to break something in myself to make a story feel real. That's where my debut came from, and the stories I've felt most proud of until now. Beneath the Urban Stars was my way of proving to myself that emotion doesn't have to come from destruction, that I didn't need to retraumatize myself to be inspired.

It began as something quick that I ironically would write while on the bus to work, and later became something rebuilt with intense amounts of care. Coming back to these characters felt like returning to people I never learned how to love, until now.

Jasper and Chiara are imperfect, complicated, and still learning how to exist in the world and with each other. They deserved the patience and attention it took to tell their story again, properly, this time.

This is not a story about fixing everything or arriving at perfect answers. Who even has perfect answers in the first place? I wanted to focus on living alongside the questions, accepting that wanting, struggling, and loving imperfectly are not failures. Our protagonists don't have everything figured out, but they have each other, and sometimes that's enough to keep going.

While writing, I imagined readers who feel a little lost, people who notice the magic in ordinary moments and refuse to give up on wanting more from life. If you see yourself anywhere in this story, I hope it feels less like a mirror and more like company.

You deserve to be loved exactly as you are.

Acknowledgements

This book exists because of the people who believed in it long before it was finished.

Thank you to **Lynn** and **Andrei**, who supported this story in its earliest, messiest draft and helped me see the diamond in the rough it already was.

Thank you to my boyfriend, **CJ**, for being there in every way that matters. For teaching me that it's possible to be loved authentically, and that life can be more than just misery. For grounding me, for loving me, and for being part of this story in ways that go far beyond the page.

Thank you to my editor, for believing in me and for loving these characters as much as I do. Your care and trust made this book what it is.

Thank you to **Arkady** and **Nai**, for always being there for every new idea, every wild concept, every story I want to write next.

And thank you to my found family, my bees. Thank you **Marissa**, **Claire**, **Monika**, **Ndenda**, **Bridget**, **Millie**. You showed me that it's possible to survive the impossible when you have a support system that truly has your back.

Finally, thank **you**! You, and every reader who has supported me from the beginning.

If you're reading this, you're part of why this book exists.

About the author

Beatrice Lebrun writes the kind of stories that make people cry, scream, or whisper "I shouldn't relate to this." She's an author and illustrator obsessed with emotional horror, queer longing, and the quiet devastation of being alive.

Born in Venezuela and now based in the U.S., Beatrice grew up living in another world entirely. Dealing with intense maladaptive daydreaming since a very young age, she spent her childhood caught between realities: one mundane and expected, the other wild, dangerous, and hers. When the world demanded she stay grounded, she turned to writing, just to keep the other realities alive.

Her protagonists are raw, flawed, and cathartic reflections of her own wounds. When she's not writing about cursed love and broken dreams, she's helping others do the same as the Creative Director of StoryForge, where she builds safe spaces for writers and stories that don't fit the mold.

You'll usually find her drawing, dancing, dreaming, or whispering to her characters like they're real people. (Sometimes, they whisper back.)

Keep in touch

Still feeling the *pull* of Beneath the Urban Stars?

Craving more longing, more obsession, more beautifully unstable characters?

If you want to step deeper into this world, visit the B.U.S. section of my website, where you'll find bonus content, freebies, and ways to linger a little longer with the story; including the companion fragrance inspired by this book, created to capture its mood, memory, and desire! You can also subscribe to my newsletter there for behind-the-scenes notes, updates, and future projects.

beatricelebrunauthor.com/b-u-s

And if you're ready for something darker and more surreal, you can find Glowrot, my debut novel, waiting for you as well! If BUS lives in the space between dreaming and waking, Glowrot dives straight into the rot of obsession, identity, and devotion that turns in on itself.

beatricelebrunauthor.com/glowrot

Don't forget to also follow me on social media (@beatrice_lebrun) to stay updated on upcoming releases, secret projects, and maybe the occasional meltdown.

Thank you for reading.

Thank you for wanting more..

www.ingramcontent.com/pod-product-compliance
Lightning Source LLC
LaVergne TN
LVHW091543070526
838199LV00002B/184